ISBN - 978-0-6399870-1-9

This is a work of fiction. Names, characters, businesses, places, events, locales, and incidents are either the products of the author's imagination or used in a fictitious manner. Any resemblance to actual persons, living or dead, or actual events is purely coincidental.

Cover and Interior design by Dazzling Designs

Proofing by Illuminate Author Services

Prologue

BRETT

"BRETT, JUST DRIVE."

Next to me, Kenzie seemed uncharacteristically nervous for what I presumed was a routine traffic stop. She tried to hide it, but I saw her hands tremble in her lap.

"Kenzie?" I stole a quick glance in my side mirror and noticed that the officer had yet to step out of the patrol car. I had a minute, at best, to get to the bottom of my girlfriend's weird behavior.

Kenzie shifting in her seat drew my attention back to her. I frowned when I saw that her blue eyes glistened with unshed tears. "Brett," she pleaded. "*Please*? I can't get arrested; my dad will kill me."

Arrested? What was she talking about? We were heading back to my apartment after a small get-together with friends. I made sure not to drink, and I wasn't driving over the speed limit. So, why the hell would she think we'd get arrested?

"Kenzie," I said again, firmer this time. "What the hell is going on?"

Those tears that had threatened to fall earlier came running down her cheeks, thick and heavy. Her bottom lip wobbled, and I saw her work down a swallow before she squeaked out, "I'm sorry, I was going to tell you." She swiped at her tears, to no avail; they just kept spilling from her eyes.

My heart dipped, and nervous tension licked its way down my spine. "Tell me what?"

She slipped her hand into the back pocket of her jeans and pulled out a bag filled with a bunch of white pills. Still crying, she stared at the packet in her palm.

"What's that?" The harsh tone of my voice caused her to jump in her seat. There was no time to feel bad because if that was what I thought it was, we *were* in trouble.

Kenzie's gaze slowly lifted to mine before dropping to the bag again. "It's methylphenidate, it helps me study."

There was a slam of a door, and a quick glance in the mirror confirmed that the officer was heading our way. I had zero time to think it through. Holding my hand palm up, I demanded, "Give it here."

"What? Why?"

"Dammit Kenzie," I gritted out. "Give me the damn bag."

We didn't have time for her to be hesitant, I reached forward and snatched the bag from her. When she turned her frown to me, I insisted, "You know nothing about this bag, got it?"

Before she could answer, there was a tap against my window. The instant I spotted the officer I knew why we were pulled over in the first place. All hopes of getting out of this mess immediately dissolved.

Gregory Heart and I did not see eye to eye at all. The disdain we felt for each other traced all the way back to high school. When I'd caught him trying to spike a girl's drink, I'd handled it the only way I knew how—with my fists. But because his daddy was the chief of police, I had been the one in trouble.

Officer Heart tapped against the window again. I placed my hand over Kenzie's trembling ones in her lap. "It's going to be okay, Sweetheart. I'll never let anything bad happen to you." I rolled down the window only to be blinded by the bright ball of light coming from Gregory's flashlight.

"Would you mind stepping out of the vehicle, *Brett*?" A sense of foreboding tugged at my spine; I just knew trouble was on the horizon.

I gave my girl one last reassuring look before I opened my door and unfolded myself from my car. Outside, the asshat smirked knowingly at me before shining his light in Kenzie's direction. "Hey Kenzie, you alright?"

I couldn't hear her answer, I only saw Gregory nod. A second later, his flashlight was trained on me again. "Did you know you have a broken taillight?"

"Pretty sure it's not broken, Gregory."

"That's officer to you, asshole." He let out a sinister chuckle before he moved to the back of my car. I was still blinking away the tiny stars when I heard the loud smash of glass shattering followed by, "Well, it is now."

Kenzie let out a mortified scream, but just as I ducked inside to console her, Gregory yelled, "Hands where I can see them!"

I raised my hands—when all I wanted to do was break this asshole's face—and slowly turned around. A second later his flashlight blinded me again.

"You been drinking tonight?"

I squinted and held my hand above my eyes as a shield. Flashing red and blue light was already slicing through the blackness of the night, I didn't need this idiot's light in my eyes too. "No, *Officer*," I hissed through clenched teeth.

Finally, Gregory switched off his flashlight and slipped it into its place on his belt. He then proceeded to put me through a number of sobriety tests even though the breathalyzer showed I had no alcohol in my system.

He did all of this in front of the car, I had no doubt he was trying to humiliate me in front of Kenzie. But it didn't bug me in the slightest. The only thing that got to me was the terrified look I saw in my girl's eyes the few times I stole a glance at her.

"Turn around, hands on the vehicle," Gregory suddenly demanded.

"What?"

"Did you think I was just going to take your word for it when you said you had no concealed weapons or drugs on your person?"

Shit. My heart jackhammered against my ribcage. For a minute there, I thought we were in the clear.

"Are you hard of hearing?" Gregory sneered.

I bit the inside of my cheek until the metallic taste of blood filled my mouth. There was no use in digging a deeper hole for myself by telling this asshole exactly what I thought of him. I raised my hands, palms facing Gregory before I slowly turned around and planted them on the hood of my car.

I locked eyes with Kenzie through the windshield, and I could tell she was debating on whether she should get out or not. I held her gaze while subtly shaking my head. She was right; her daddy would be beside himself if she got arrested.

He owned a PR company and had some pretty famous and influential clients. He wouldn't take kindly to his daughter smearing the family name. Mr. Michaels was already looking down his nose at his daughter for dating an art student.

I kept my focus on my girl while Gregory started to frisk me. It didn't take him long to find what he was looking for. "Do you have a prescription for these?" He asked way too cheery as he dangled the bag in front of my face.

"No," was my flat reply.

"Well, then I'm going to have to take your ass to the precinct. Hands behind your back."

The sob that broke free from Kenzie's throat tore through my heart. I wanted nothing more than to wrap my arms around her and pull her into my chest. She was my entire world, and there was nothing I wouldn't do for her. Where I came from, you protected the ones you loved, no questions asked.

The cold metal circling my wrists brought me back to reality. Instead of pulling me to my feet, he leaned over me and whispered, "You know, with you gone, that girl of yours is going to need someone to keep her bed warm," his arm on my back pressed me deeper into the hood. "But don't worry, I'm only too happy to be of service. I mean who wouldn't want a piece of that perfect—"

The rest of his sentence was lost to the night air as I jerked back, and my head connected with his. I ignored the sharp pain shooting through my skull as I started to twist my body around, ready to finish what I started. "You go near her, I'll kill you!"

With my hands clasped behind my back, I had no way to defend myself against the blow that came courtesy of Gregory's police-issued baton. The pain in my head multiplied, and I was helpless when he slammed me back down on the hood.

"Now, that little stunt is sure to earn you some extra jail time."

My eyes locked onto Kenzie's, and for a split-second, everything else disappeared. With one look, I tried to reassure her that everything was going to be okay even though I knew it wasn't. I kept my gaze on her as long as I could while Gregory led me to the squad car.

Little did I know that would be the last time I saw my girl.

KENZIE

12 years later.

"ARE YOU FREAKING KIDDING ME?"

I pressed the button to the right of the steering wheel, only to have the engine of my car stutter before it died. With a heavy sigh, I took in my surroundings. There was nothing but bluebonnets for miles to my left and right; the only sign of life were the birds flocking to who-knows-where.

I poked at my phone mounted to the dash and pulled up my maps application; I needed to know where I was before I called for assistance. I scrolled once, twice, and then stopped.

No.

The nearest town was Willow Creek, and it also happened to be the only town in the world I wanted to avoid like the plague. I scrolled some more; there had to be another town.

"Ugh! Seriously!?" I sounded as exasperated as I felt. If I didn't want to be stranded there for at least another few hours, I had no other choice than to call a towing service in Willow Creek.

I pulled my bottom lip between my teeth while I searched for a number I could call. Funny how life liked to kick you when you were down. It wasn't usual for me to drive hundreds of miles to meet with a client, but things had happened, and I needed the time to think.

Finally, I found a number for an auto shop. I dialed it; the man on the other end of the line assured me he'd be there in less than an hour. When I hung up, I pulled up a familiar number on my phone, but for some reason, I was hesitant to press the little green button.

And that there was precisely why I needed time to think. The typical reaction to your boyfriend asking you to move in with him should be excitement. It shouldn't scare you to the point where you jump in your car and drive for miles and miles.

And it definitely shouldn't make you hesitant to phone him when you'd landed in a crisis.

Instead of dialing Dean, I punched in my best friend, Zoe's number. She answered on the third ring.

"Kenz, hi." She sounded a bit breathless, and I was terrified to ask what I'd interrupted. Zoe was all for living in the moment; she even had the words *'carpe diem'* tattooed on her wrist.

"Uh, is this a bad time?"

There was shuffling, I heard faint whispering before Zoe said, "Don't be silly."

"My car broke down right in front of Willow Creek." The words came out along with the whoosh of breath that left my lungs. Zoe was the only person who knew why being stranded in Willow Creek, even just for an afternoon, was mortifying.

"What? Okay, you have to backtrack… I thought you were flying down on Monday? What's this about your car breaking down?"

I ran my thumb over my lip and stared at the endless amount of blue stretching as far as the eye could see. "Dean wants me to move in with him."

"Oh. And your natural reaction to that was to jump in your car and get as far away from him as possible?"

Hearing it like that made me sound like a bad person. "I'm horrible," defeated, I dropped my head to the steering wheel.

"You're being dramatic," I heard the smile in my friend's voice. There was a short moment of silence before Zoe continued, "Maybe this isn't such a bad thing, Kenz."

"Yeah?" I asked, my voice thick with sarcasm. "How do you figure that?"

"Look—" not fazed by my mordacity, Zoe went on, "—first of all, there is a hell of a chance that you won't be in Willow Creek long enough to run into him—"

"But—"

"If you do, you might be able to finally get some closure. Kenz, I know you don't want to hear this; but I'm gonna say it, anyway."

I lifted my head and stared at the endless stretch of land before me while I waited for her to continue.

"You need to let go of the past, so you can focus on your future."

She was right. Keeping tabs on your old boyfriend wasn't healthy. In my defense, I was only doing it so I'd know which towns to avoid.

Yeah, that's my story, and I'm sticking to it.

"Kenz, you still there?"

"Mmm hmm." A rumble drew my attention to the road just in time for me to see a truck come to a standstill in front of me. "I think help has arrived. I'll call you as soon as I know what's happening."

A giggle filtered through the line before Zoe's reply, "Uh, maybe text first."

I couldn't help but laugh as I shook my head and hung up. Most people thought of Zoe as an easy girl, but the sad truth was her level of detachment stemmed from something that most people wouldn't survive. I didn't always agree with her choices, but hell if I was going to condemn her for them.

I had all the hope in the world that one of these days a guy worth her time was going to stick around long enough to be the salve that heals all her broken pieces. The slam of a door pulled me from my reverie and drew my attention back to the problem at hand.

A giant of a man, covered in tattoos emerged from the truck. I was about to lock my doors and dial 911 when the excited squeal of a child stole my attention. Where the tattooed man was big, with tanned skin, dark hair, and an even darker beard, the little boy bouncing up and down next to him was the exact opposite.

A mop of winter-white hair covered his head, and his pale skin made me want to offer him a tube of sunscreen. As striking as their differences were, it was the undeniable affection between them that stole my breath.

The man crouched before the boy and said something that had his smile growing by the second. After a quick ruffle of the boy's hair, the man stood and pulled the boy in for a hug.

I didn't know why my mind went where it did when I saw that, but the only thing I could think of was how my relationship with my father wasn't anything like that. Another laugh broke free as I imagined how my mother would react if I brought a guy home that looked like that man.

I stepped out of the car when they reached me. I wasn't a short girl, plus I was wearing four-inch heels and still the guy towered above me.

"Hey there," I gave them a small wave.

"Hello," the excitement I saw on his face came through in the boy's voice. Tattooed Giant lightly nudged the boy with his hip which prompted him to add, "Ma'am." This child was way too cute for his own good.

A soft chuckle drew my attention back to the giant whose ink-covered hand was stretched out, "Afternoon, ma'am. This here is Flynn, I'm Logan. What seems to be the problem?"

After shaking Logan's hand, I bent down and shook Flynn's too. The way his cheeks turned rosy was the most adorable thing I'd seen in a long time.

"It just died on me," I explained when I straightened.

"May I?" Logan nudged his head in the direction of my car.

"Please."

I stood next to Flynn, and we watched Logan reach into the car and pop my Mazda's hood. He checked a few things in the engine before the cracking sound of the hood being closed filled the air.

"I think it might be your starter, or by the looks of this water puddle—" he pointed to the road, "—your radiator. I'll know more once I've thoroughly checked it over at the shop."

My heart rate kicked up as panic rushed through my veins. I flicked my wrist to check the time. "And, uh, how long will that take?"

Logan ran a hand over his beard, "Hard to say, but if it's only a fuse problem, you can be on your way before nightfall."

"If it's not?"

"Well, then it's a whole other story. I'll have to order parts, and your car will probably be at the shop for a few days—"

"A few days?" I squeaked out.

He walked over to Flynn and placed both his hands on the boy's shoulders, "Let's not get ahead of ourselves, ma'am—"

"Kenzie."

He gave me a small nod, "Kenzie, let me drop you off at the diner and I promise by the time you've finished your coffee or tea I'll have a solid answer for you."

"If it's all the same, I'd like to wait."

Logan frowned and by the way his eyes narrowed, I could tell he thought I didn't trust him with my car. I wasn't going to correct him. I'd rather he thought that than admit to a stranger that I don't want to sit in a diner because I'm afraid I'd run into my ex.

With my Mazda hooked, we started the short drive to Willow Creek. The closer we got, the more nervous I became. By the time we drove past the '*Welcome*' sign, my heart was pumping to a frantic rhythm.

"You're stuck here."

I almost choked at the sound of those three words. Logan straightened from where he was bent over my car's engine and wiped his hands with a rag he pulled from his back pocket. "For a few days, at least," he added.

I shook my head and pinched the bridge of my nose. That was the last thing I needed.

"I'm sorry I don't have better news," he sounded sincere.

My lips pulled into a tight smile, "Yeah, me too." I aimlessly scanned my surroundings and asked, "If you can give me directions to the nearest hotel, that would be great." What I needed was a long, hot bath and to get our potential client to reschedule our meeting.

"Hotel?" Logan chuckled. "No hotel, but we do have a pretty decent guesthouse here." He then grabbed his phone from the bench behind him and stepped away to make a call.

I folded my arms in front of me and did a slow perusal of the auto shop. I spotted Flynn in the far corner, playing games on his tablet. He was such an adorable little boy, and the easy exchanges between him and Logan were absolutely heart-melting.

"All set. Mrs. Davis has a room for you."

The suddenness of his voice had me jumping on the spot; I barely resisted the urge to press my palm to my heart. "Mrs. Davis?" I asked.

"Yeah," he let out a short whistle which drew Flynn's attention. After Logan beckoned him with a quick jerk of his head, the boy jumped up and hurried toward us. "She's the owner of the guesthouse," Logan continued. "C'mon, we'll drop you off."

Twenty minutes later, I was 'checked-in' and standing in the middle of a pale green and yellow room wondering what else could possibly go wrong.

BRETT

I SAT IN THE DRIVEWAY WITH MY FINGERS CURLED AROUND THE STEERING WHEEL in a white-knuckled grip, silently willing the strange feeling that had taken over to go away. I was perfectly happy with my life. So, where the empty feeling—that I only felt in my best friend and his fiancée's presence—came from was anyone's guess.

I just knew it was unwelcome.

After I took a few fortifying breaths, I climbed out of my truck. With my six-pack tucked under my arm and flowers in hand, I bypassed the front door and made my way down the side path that led to the back of the house.

Not long after they'd gotten engaged, my friends realized that they needed a bigger place. They both agreed that they wanted to be closer to Logan's parents. As luck would have it, a property near the Jackson ranch was for sale, but it needed some touching up. If you asked me, I'd choose a house outside of town that needed work, over one in town that didn't, every single time.

I side-stepped a few building materials to push my way through the side gate.

"You made it," I couldn't help but grin when I spotted Harper rushing toward me, their Rottweiler tailing behind her. Deciding his human-mom was taking far too long; Dozer bolted around her and made a beeline for me.

Digging my heels in, I braced for the doggy kisses I was about to receive, but they never came. A sharp whistle stopped the dog in his tracks. "No, Dozer." Harper admonished. "Go play." I'd seen her work her magic on him countless times, but it never ceased to amaze me. "Logan and Flynn will be here soon," she huffed out.

I pulled her into a side hug when she finally reached me. "For you," she took the colorful bouquet I held out and gave them a generous sniff. A low, drawn-out whistle blew over my lips as I slowly scanned their backyard. "The guys are making progress."

The amount of work that had been done in a little under a year was absolutely astonishing. Not only did they tear down the main house and build a new one, but they'd also added a swimming pool and a huge play area for Flynn too.

"They are," I was drawn back to the present by Harper tugging on my arm and pulling me toward the house. "And once they're done, we'll have that backyard wedding Logan can't seem to shut up about." She shook her head, but I knew that she was just as excited as my friend.

It had taken me a while to warm up to Harper. You could blame my own life experiences for my skepticism. You know the saying: *Fool me once, shame on you. Fool me twice, shame on me?*

Well, I'd already been fooled once, and I wasn't stupid enough to walk down that path again.

When we stepped into the kitchen, Harper pulled a vase from one of the cupboards. After she placed the flowers in the center of the breakfast nook, she took the room-temperature beers from me and replaced them with an ice cold one from her fridge. I unscrewed it and immediately gulped down half of the yeasty brew.

I looked to my left where Harper was staring at me with a perplexed look on her face.

"You okay? Something about you seems off." She folded her arms in front of her and tilted her head to the side.

It was a little unsettling that she'd noticed. This gnawing feeling that kept eating at my gut probably stemmed from my restless night. Every once in a while my dreams would be haunted by the only woman who'd ever breached the walls around my heart. Her blue eyes always mocking me with the fake love shining in them, her gorgeous mouth always spewing lies I'd believed.

Yeah, something was off alright, but that was nobody's business but mine. "I'm good." I gave her a wink, but I could tell she wasn't buying it.

Her mouth opened but whatever she was about to say was lost to the excited giggle that traveled through the house. A second later, Flynn came bouncing into the kitchen, looking like a kid who'd just been let loose in a candy store.

"Flynn, my man," I dropped to my haunches and held up my hand. "Up top."

He smacked my palm, and his little face lit up as he proceeded to tell me about the afternoon he'd had with Logan. "Really, red?" I enthusiastically inquired when he told me about the super cool car—his words—they towed to the shop.

"Mmm hmm, yeah," he confirmed by furiously nodding his head. "And the lady was really pretty," he whipped his head around, "But not as pretty as you, Mommy." Without pausing to take a breath, he turned his attention back to me, the words rushing from his lips, "And she was wearing these pointy shoes that—"

In my peripheral vision, I caught sight of Logan pulling Harper to him and touching his lips to hers. That unwelcome empty feeling crashed down on my chest so hard and fast, I just about suffocated. I was happy for my friends, I really was, but I didn't want what they had. I'd tried my hand at love once and not only did my heart get stomped on, I'd lost my freedom too.

So, why in the hell did this feeling feel a lot like envy?

"Hey buddy," Logan's voice grabbed both my and Flynn's attention. "Why don't you go get Dozer's new toy out of the truck and show it to him?"

Another excited giggle filtered through the room as Flynn bolted back the way he came. With a shake of my head, I pushed to my feet and emptied the rest of my beer. Logan dropped another kiss to Harper's lips before he pulled two more beers from the fridge and handed me one.

"You should've called me," I said as I followed him outside. "I could've handled the tow." We settled on the newly built deck that overlooked their spacious backyard.

"Nah," Logan answered after a long swallow of beer. "Besides, I like taking Flynn out on a call with me."

Even though they didn't share the same DNA, Logan loved that boy as if he were his own. That love was returned tenfold.

"Tell me about this *'really cool car'* that has Flynn so mesmerized."

A chuckle sounded from beside me. "I'm not sure if he's taken by the car or the girl." My friend shifted, so he was facing me, amusement all over his face. "But unfortunately for my little man, I don't think Miss. Mazda will be sticking around too long." He brought his beer to his lips, and after another long swig he murmured, "Those rich, city types never do."

I lifted my shoulder in a shrug, "Guess we're making her car priority, so she can get out of our town."

Logan let out a hum of approval, and we turned our attention to Dozer and Flynn playing tug-of-war with the dog's new toy. The silence that filled the air around us was as comfortable as it was familiar. I didn't have a brother, in fact, I didn't have any family left—not blood related, anyway. My best friend was as close to a brother as I was gonna get and in moments like these, I felt like I belonged somewhere.

I heard their home phone ring, and a few minutes later Harper appeared on the deck, holding a beer and water. "You're driving." She handed me the bottled water before slipping onto Logan's lap and wrapping her arms around his neck. "Have you asked him?"

Asked me what?

He chuckled and pulled her even closer to him, "I'm getting to it, Sugar." Then he turned his attention to me, "We were hoping you'd use your glass blowing skills for our wedding."

I'd happened upon the art at a festival I'd attended with my old college girlfriend. We'd spent hours watching the man manipulate the molten glass and creating the most beautiful things. In an instant, I'd known what I wanted to do with my life. I was well on my way to realizing that dream when the ground got ripped from beneath me.

Swallowing the bile that rose in my throat, I mustered a half-smile, "Whatever you need."

Harper's smile went all the way up to her green eyes, "Thank you! So, are we seeing you at the ranch tomorrow?"

I shook my head while I toyed with the bottle in my hands. "I'm having lunch at the guesthouse."

"Interesting." My friend remarked tentatively.

I glared at Logan, "What's so *interesting* about that exactly?"

Harper poked Logan in the chest and shook her head. To me, she said, "We'll miss you, but we'll stop by tomorrow night with dessert." I didn't even know when it had happened, but somewhere during the past year we'd started getting together on Sunday and Monday nights.

Sunday nights were what you'd call family night, or as I liked to call it, dessert Sunday. All of us—Logan and his brothers along with Harper and Lizzy and the kids — got together at someone's place and stuffed our faces with pie while our competitive sides came out during board games.

Monday nights were for the adults. The kids would have a sleepover at Logan's parents while the grownups enjoyed a night out at Joe's, our local haunt.

"I'm going to go see what those two are up to," Harper announced. She laughed as she slipped off her man's lap. "There is nothing more sinister than a quiet kid and an equally quiet dog." Shaking her head, she walked toward Flynn and Dozer.

"You've been spending a lot of time with Lola lately," Logan remarked while his gaze remained on Harper.

"Mrs. Davis invited me over, not Lola." My comeback was weak, and I knew it. In my defense though, when a sweet old lady offered you a home cooked meal, you didn't decline. The fact that her granddaughter and I took the odd tumble between the sheets had nothing to do with me accepting her invitation.

"Look, man," the seriousness in my friend's voice gave me an uneasy feeling. "I know this thing with her is casual for *you*, but does *she* see it that way?"

My jaw clenched in irritation, but to be fair, my pissy mood had nothing to do with Logan baiting me over Lola. The way he never gave up on Harper—no matter how much shit we gave him—had my mind running to the only woman I ever loved.

As much as I wanted to believe that love conquered all, I was proof that it also destroyed everything.

"Lola knows what we are and she's good with that," I pushed to my feet. "We grilling some steaks or what?" It looked like my friend had more to say, but he had the good sense not to voice any of it.

By the time I drove home, I was craving the solitude of my cabin. The deeper I traveled into the woods, the calmer my soul felt. I'd tried living in town for a while, but after spending four years of my life in prison, I needed a place where no fence was necessary.

It took some decent negotiating, but I'd managed to buy a piece of land a few miles outside of town. Nothing could ever compare to having the woodland for a backyard.

I rolled to a stop in my usual parking space and headed inside my spacious log cabin. With a long sigh, I shrugged out of my jacket and toed off my boots. I pulled my tee over my head and caught sight of the tiny butterflies. From their spot on my bookcase, they mocked me.

Heavy feet carried me across the room, the hole in my chest grew with every step. Glass butterflies took up almost a third of the space on my wall-to-wall case. Different colors, different sizes scattered about. I ran a finger over the wings of the blue one closest to me.

One of these days I would be able to look at them without the sting of betrayal or misery flooding my heart.

Today was not that day.

KENZIE

TWENTY-SEVEN.

The number of blocks that were on the ceiling. There were also tiny cracks in the two middle blocks and in the one right above my head.

Eighteen hand-painted pink roses decorated the white-wash furniture.

Sixty-two pale yellow vertical and horizontal lines crisscrossed to create small squares on the green wallpaper.

I knew these things because I'd spent my night tossing and turning, and apparently, counting everything I could. Not even the melatonin I'd taken could keep me asleep for longer than an hour at a time.

At least I had one less thing to worry about. My potential client, Carly Williams, had agreed to reschedule our meeting. I rolled onto my side and huffed out a breath. Staring at the white curtains, I willed them to give me answers to the questions that floated around in my head.

Bzz Bzz

I clutched my chest and glared at my vibrating phone on the nightstand. A quick peek confirmed it was Dean calling… again. My heart drummed to a nervous rhythm, and instead of answering his call, I slipped out of bed and marched to the bathroom.

Pulling the curtain back, I reached inside the shower and turned on the faucet. While I slipped out of my shorts and cami, my tired reflection stopped me cold. After I curled my fingers around the smooth ceramic of the basin, I leaned forward and studied my appearance up close.

I looked as forlorn as I felt. Puffy cheeks and dark smudges beneath my eyes, evidence of my lack of sleep. I hadn't even bothered to wash my makeup off last night. I hadn't looked that pitiful since college, only then my scattered appearance had had nothing to do with sleep deprivation. A deep frown formed on my forehead and anger bubbled its way through my veins. Twelve years was a long time. Long enough to let go of your past.

Why the hell couldn't I let go then?

I shook my head and stepped beneath the scalding water. Tilting my head, I put my face directly in the path of the warm spray. Seconds morphed into minutes as I just stood and allowed the water to draw the stress from my limbs.

Eventually, I grabbed a sponge, cleaned myself and turned off the shower. It was when I was sitting on the bed, towel-drying my hair, that I realized Zoe was right.

I needed closure.

My heart could never fully let go of Brett because of that awful letter that just didn't resonate with the man I so passionately loved. The man who took the blame for me.

My cellphone buzzed to life again, giving me a heart attack in the process. Dropping the towel, I leaned over the bed to snatch my phone from the nightstand. I closed my eyes and took a deep breath before I answered.

"Babe, where have you been?" Dean's voice greeted me. "I've been calling since yesterday."

Guilt ate at me because of my behavior. Dean was the kind of man that every woman wanted. He was handsome, came from a good family and along with his steady job, he had values I respected.

"I had car trouble and—"

"Yeah, I know," he cut in, sounding more hurt than angry. "Your dad phoned me last night."

After I'd taken a few minutes to decompress last night, I texted Zoe—who still hadn't responded—then I made a quick call to my parents. It didn't surprise me when they weren't happy with me. My mother was absolutely mortified when she learned I'd be spending a few nights in a place that didn't have room service. The only thing my father was worried about was whether we could get Carly to agree to see me at another time.

"Oh." I slipped off the bed and walked over to the drawn curtains. Delicately pulling them back, I peeked outside. "I didn't want to worry you," I answered weakly while I stared at Mrs. Davis's beautiful backyard. My attention was immediately drawn to the gazebo situated in the far left corner. With all the colorful flowers surrounding it, I bet there'd be tons of butterflies floating around.

"That makes no sense, Kenzie." Dean's voice sliced through my thoughts. "We're in a relationship, I should be your first call when you're in trouble." I imagined him running a hand through his blond hair—like he always did when he was at a loss. "This is about me asking you to move in with me, isn't it?" He added softly.

I let go of the curtain and turned so I could lean my back against the wall. With my index and middle fingers, I circled my temple repeatedly. "Dean, can we not do this now?"

A defeated sigh filtered through the line. "When will you be back?"

"I don't know."

"Do you want me to come there?"

"That's not necessary. Besides, don't you have to be in court on Monday?" Dean was a criminal defense lawyer, a good one too. So good, that he'd already made junior partner.

"Jonah knows the case like the back of his hand, he can lead."

I threw my head back and squeezed my eyes shut. "You've been preparing for this case for months. Dean, you should lead. And I'm pretty sure my car won't take that long, anyway."

"Kenzie," I spotted the smallest hint of anger in his voice. "Why do I get the feeling that you don't want me there?"

"It's not that, it's just—" I opened my eyes and stared at the ceiling while I struggled to find the right words to say. A knock sounded, and I welcomed the out. "There's someone at the door, I'll call you later."

Dean's clipped, "Goodbye," made me feel both sad and relieved. My brows drew together while I stared at the phone in my hand.

Another knock stole my attention. I dropped my phone on the bed and headed for the door. On the other side stood a woman that looked like she'd stepped out of a 50s magazine. With her shiny black hair intricately knotted on top of her head and lips painted bright red, she probably turned heads wherever she went.

"Hi, I'm Lola."

I smiled and gripped her outstretched hand, "Kenzie." Colorful patterns coiled around her arm all the way to her collarbone. There was even more ink peeking out from beneath her white crop top. *Is everyone in Willow Creek covered in tattoos?*

Her assessing gaze traveled from my silk blouse to my pencil skirt and down to my bare feet. I got the impression that she was sizing me up. "Nana wanted to know if you'll be joining us for lunch today."

I'd briefly met Mrs. Davis last night, she was friendly and welcoming. Having lunch with her hardly seemed like a hardship. "I'd love to, thanks."

After Lola informed me that lunch was served at one, she disappeared down the hall. I closed the door and walked over to the dresser next to the window. Tilting my head to the side, I tried to see myself through a stranger's eyes. My white blouse neatly tucked into my black skirt looked professional but probably screamed *stuck-up* to most.

My gaze flitted to my heels, still lying in the same spot I'd kicked them off last night before it slowly traveled to my open suitcase perched on the couch. I groaned because I knew it contained nothing but business attire. Mother would probably have a fit if her daughter traipsed around in jeans and a tee.

I could already hear her: *'You only have one chance to make a first impression, Kenzie. Your clothes should reflect your sophistication.'*

With that thought, Dean popped up in my mind. He shared my parents' view on how you presented yourself in public. I looked up at the ceiling, trying to recall a time where I'd seen him out in public wearing jeans.

Never. Slacks and a dress shirt was his idea of dressing down.

I tried my best to shake my depressed mood, but by the time I headed down for lunch, I was even more wired than I'd been when my car broke down. Pausing at the entrance of the dining room, I inhaled the delicious smell that permeated the air before I forced a smile and entered.

The space was so different from what I was accustomed to. In the middle of the room stood a big farm-style dining table, warm and welcoming. I suspected the mouthwatering aromas came from the buffet table to the left. My stomach chose that moment to remind me of how little food it'd had since yesterday. I pressed my hand against my belly as I ventured further, scanning my surroundings with every step.

To the right were three bright yellow loveseats arranged in front of the window that overlooked the backyard. I heard movement and turned my head to the table where Mrs. Davis stood smiling.

She'd just placed a small vase containing flowers on the table, and she was admiring them. I felt like a towering giant when I reached her. She had to be about a foot shorter than my five-foot-seven.

"They're beautiful," I said in lieu of a greeting. "Are they from your garden?"

The older woman beamed up at me; her chocolate eyes shining brightly. "They are," she twisted her plump body so she could fully face me. "Did you sleep well, dear?"

"Like the dead," I lied.

Mrs. Davis looked me up and down and then shook her head, "There was no need to dress up for lunch."

I felt like a complete idiot. Heat crept up my neck and settled on my cheeks. "I, uh—"

"Nana, I can't find the—" Lola burst into the room. "—cinnamon." She'd changed into a sleeveless form-fitting red number that ended about mid-thigh. She looked so stunning, *I* felt underdressed.

A soft laugh sounded from beside me, "Top shelf, my sweet Lola." With a muttered thanks, Lola ducked back the way she came. Mrs. Davis touched her palm to the back of my arm, "Come on, let's sit for a bit while we wait for Lola's *friend* to arrive."

We seated ourselves on the couches by the window. The pops of color that burst through the green were simply magnificent to see. I could imagine someone losing hours by just sitting there, staring out the window.

"The garden used to be my Gerald's favorite place," Mrs. Davis's voice was soft and wistful.

When I turned to her and saw the dreamy expression on her face, I almost didn't want to speak, afraid I'd interrupt whatever memory she was lost in. "I can see why." My voice was just above a whisper.

The doorbell sounded and a few seconds after that, Lola's cheery, "I'll get it," filled the air. That pulled the older woman from her reverie.

Mrs. Davis's smile lit up her whole face. "Ah, young love." She reached over and placed her hand over mine. "Do you have a love waiting for you at home, dear?"

Did I? "I—"

"Is that your famous roast I smell, Mrs. D?"

My blood turned to ice, and my heart flatlined before it kicked up again at an alarming pace.

That voice.

After twelve years of not hearing it, the deep, silky timbre still managed to send chills down my spine.

My gaze skittered to the dining room entrance, and the breath rushed from my lungs. Across the room, our eyes locked and as much as I wanted to—*needed to*—look away, I couldn't. A gasp tried to work its way up my throat, but I swallowed it down.

I was vaguely aware of Mrs. Davis talking to me, but I couldn't hear a word she was saying. My attention was firmly fixed on one person and one person alone.

Brett Carter.

BRETT

WHAT THE—

My brain short-circuited, and the breath left my lungs as I tried to make sense of what, or rather who, I was looking at. It had to be a dream. A *beautiful* nightmare. I wanted to blink her away, but some invisible force kept my lids from closing.

Kenzie.

If it was at all possible, she was even more beautiful than the last time I'd seen her. The day she'd ripped my heart out and ruined me. What was left of that thing inside my chest ached at the sight of her. She was akin to a poisonous flower; soft on the eyes but detrimental to the soul.

"Brett?"

The confusion in Lola's voice broke the spell I was under, and I was granted the reprieve I so desperately needed when I could finally shut my eyes—even if it was just for a few seconds. When

I opened them again, I fully expected Kenzie's gaze to be anywhere but on me.

I was wrong.

Her hypnotizing blue depths started to pull me in once more. Lola uttered my name again, and my focus slowly shifted to her. Deep lines marred her forehead and her jaw ticked in irritation. "What was that?" I managed to ask. That invisible pull forced my attention back to Kenzie who looked as if she was ready to dispel her breakfast. *You and me both.*

"Do you two know each other?" Lola did nothing to hide her annoyance.

Still holding Kenzie's gaze, I tilted my head slightly. I swear she held her breath while everyone waited for my answer. "Know is a rather strong word," I heard the ice in my tone. "We're…acquainted." Even from across the room I saw hurt flash on her face before she schooled her features and finally, *finally*, averted her gaze.

Stings, doesn't it?

Yeah, I might've been the biggest asshole for intentionally hurting her feelings, but she'd hurt way more than just my feelings. I felt Lola's eyes burning a hole in my skull, and I had to resist the urge to hightail outta there.

"Well," Mrs. D clasped her hands together. "Food's getting cold, we should eat. Everyone must be starving."

Funny, I'd been ravenous up until a few moments ago. Now, I had no idea how I was going to do this sweet old lady's roast any justice.

I wondered if everyone else felt the tension in the air as we silently dished up and arranged ourselves around the table. Instead of taking her usual spot opposite me, Lola slipped in beside me and scooted closer. *Weird.* Too busy trying to decipher her strange behavior; I didn't notice that Kenzie took the seat across from me.

Great, how am I going to eat now?

"So," Lola drawled. "How was dinner with Harper and Logan?"

I forked a green bean and said, "Good," before shoveling it into my mouth. I knew that Mrs. D was a great cook, so the fact that the food in my mouth had no taste was no fault on her part. "The renovations are coming along."

"How exciting," Mrs. D commented. "Have they set a date yet?"

"No," I glanced at Kenzie pushing the food around on her plate. She looked uncomfortable and out of place. A sliver of sympathy tried to work its way to my heart; I squelched it down. Turning my attention back to Mrs. D, I smiled, "But I'm sure it's going to be sooner rather than later." I tried the beef, and it too was tasteless.

"Oh good, I just adore weddings." She turned her attention to Kenzie. "You never did tell me if you had someone special waiting for you at home."

The roast beef in my mouth suddenly tasted like acid. I focused on my plate while at the same time straining to hear her answer.

There was a long moment of silence before Kenzie softly stated, "I am seeing someone, yes." I detected a hint of uncertainty in her voice, but I didn't allow myself to dwell on it.

"Will you be walking down the aisle soon?"

I didn't hear Kenzie's answer because Lola chose that moment to slide a hand along my thigh; the action so sudden it startled me to the point of knocking my knee against the underside of the table. Instead of pulling away she ventured higher. Normally I didn't mind her getting frisky, but for some reason, it felt… wrong. I cleared my throat and shifted to the left, away from Lola.

The ongoing conversation opposite me ceased, two confused sets of eyes flitting between the woman to my right and me. My gaze collided with Kenzie's again, and so help me, I was helpless to look away. A cloudless sky would be envious of the particular shade of her eyes. So blue, so bright with a mixture of sadness and vulnerability swirling in them.

That look sent ice blasting through my entire body. *That* was the look I'd seen the night Gregory had pulled us over.

I couldn't breathe.

I couldn't be there.

I stood so abruptly, my chair toppled over. "I'm sorry, Mrs. D," I bent and righted the fallen piece of furniture. "I have to go." Not waiting for an answer, I rushed to the front door.

Just as my fingers curled around the handle, Lola's, "Brett, wait!" halted me. I squeezed my eyes shut and sucked in a breath. *Just let me leave.*

"Hey, what's up with you today?"

Slowly, I uncurled my fingers and pivoted. The confusion etched on her face had me thinking about Logan's concerns. I shook that thought away; I'd been upfront with her from the get-go. A relationship was the furthest thing from my mind.

"Nothing," the lie slipped from my tongue with ease.

Eyes narrowed, head tilted, she ran a finger down the center of my chest. "If you say so. Want me to come over later so you can work this *nothing* out of your system?"

I shook my head, "Not tonight, Lo." I needed to be alone.

She looked hurt, and my friend's warning rang in my ears again. It became too much. Without another word, I yanked the door open and headed for my truck.

Gently, I brushed Kenzie's hair away from her face and tucked it behind her ear. "You're so damn beautiful," I murmured against her lips. Resisting the urge to kiss her senseless, I pulled back slightly to watch the blush settle in her cheeks, and her lips lift into a shy smile.

"I love it when you look at me like that," she confessed.

"Like what?"

Kenzie's smile grew even wider. "Like I'm your entire world, and you can't bear to let me go."

I brushed my fingertips over her cheek, "You are and I can't." Pushing my fingers into her hair, I cupped the back of her head and pulled her face to mine. Against her mouth, I pleaded, "Tell me you'll always be mine?"

"Forever," feather-soft kisses stole my breath, "I'll love you forever, Brett."

"Shit!!" The wood splintered beneath my knuckles as I rammed my fist through my bedroom door. Images of Kenzie and I had been rolling through my mind like a movie stuck on repeat since I left the guesthouse. A sharp pain shot from my hand and settled in my chest.

I cursed some more.

I'd always known that I would never completely be over her. How can you ever be over someone who used to be your entire existence? You couldn't. You simply learned to function without them. And clearly, that was a lesson I had yet to master in twelve years.

How was it even possible to despise someone so much and at the same time have a burning need to pull them into your arms and never let go?

"Stop! Just stop it!!" My body vibrated with tension, and even my home couldn't offer me the calm I craved. My heart kicked up a gear, that empty suffocating feeling slamming into me at breakneck speed.

I rushed to my dresser, yanked it open and grabbed the first pair of sweatpants I could find. It took me less than a minute to strip out of my jeans and shirt to don the sweats.

Another minute later and dried leaves and twigs crushed under my feet as I raced through the woods as if the devil himself were chasing me.

Even that wasn't fast enough.

I increased my pace and wondered how long and how far I needed to run to get away from the past that wouldn't stop haunting me.

BRETT

OUT OF BREATH, I STUMBLED TO THE FRIDGE AND PULLED OUT A BOTTLE OF WATER, I swallowed down the entire thing. Out of all the places her car could break down, it happened in my damn town. Wiping the back of my hand over my mouth, I stared at the ceiling and cursed.

How was it possible that just one look into those blue depths could undo over a decade's worth of healing? The pain in my chest gnawed at me again, reminding me—no, *mocking me*—that I had just been fooling myself all these years.

I closed my eyes, and my mind immediately produced an image of Kenzie; so vivid I could almost reach out and touch her. Shit, she was beautiful! Even through a haze of anger, it was impossible not to notice. Confusion had me cursing some more. A part of me wanted to scream and shout until she owned up to her betrayal and repented. Another part—the part I currently despised—wanted to pull her to me and kiss her as if the past twelve years were nothing but a dream.

My tongue snaked over my lips, and my skin tingled, even after a decade I could still recall how sweet she'd tasted. It had taken me a long time to realize and accept that Kenzie Michaels would always be a part of me whether I wanted it or not. The number of women I'd used to try to rid myself of the memories was shameful.

Much like it had since I'd left the guesthouse, the past kept forcing itself to the present. I flattened my palms against my fridge and dropped my head to the smooth metallic surface, utter depletion seeping into my bones. I needed to focus on getting her car fixed so she could leave my damn town.

I pushed off the fridge and started for the bathroom. What I needed was a long, hot shower and possibly some quality alone time. Just as I turned into the hallway, loud banging sounded from the door. With one foot still halfway to the ground, my brows pulled together.

Who the hell could that be?

Frozen in my awkward stance, I eyed the door as if I could see through the wood. I was in no mood for company. Deciding whoever was on the other side could come back another time, I continued my trek.

I'd made it all of three steps when the banging sounded again. "What the—" With a shake of my head, I changed direction and headed toward the front of the cabin with the sole intent of telling the door-banger to piss the hell off.

I wasn't expecting to find three people standing on my deck when I yanked on the wooden barrier between me and the persistent knocker. Normally, seeing my friends' faces wouldn't fill me with the irritation currently scratching on my bones.

"Are we interrupting something?" Chase, Logan's brother, asked while all three of them took in my sweaty appearance. He was the town veterinarian and the youngest of the Jackson brothers.

"Just got back from a run."

"Are you gonna invite us in or not?" Logan's other brother, Eli, piped up. He was the oldest and the broodiest of the bunch. No one could blame his constant suspicious nature, though. Being left to raise his daughter alone, Eli Jackson's life had definitely not been all sunshine and roses.

I could relate to that.

Logan took a step forward and peeked over my shoulder. "Are you having your own kind of dessert in there? Should we take momma's pie and leave you to it?"

Shit! I'd barely laid eyes on the woman, and already she was screwing with my brain. For the first time, I'd completely forgotten about dessert Sunday. Sheepishly, I stepped to the side and allowed my friends entry. "Just the three of you, then?" I asked as the boys rushed past me.

"Yeah," Logan called from the kitchen. I shut the door and took a few deep breaths before I joined them. It never ceased to amaze me how comfortable we were in each other's spaces.

Like now, Logan was digging through my fridge while Eli busied himself with pulling plates from the cupboards. Chase was perched on a countertop digging through my mail. Yeah, we might not have shared the same DNA or last name, but these guys were my family.

I crossed my arms in front of me and propped my shoulder against the doorframe, the irritation I'd felt a mere moment ago already dissolving. "So, where are the others?"

Eli served up his mother's pecan pie. If I could choose what I wanted to have for my last meal on earth, it would be Mrs. Jackson's pie. "Molly and Flynn were too lost in their movie to tag along, and momma and Harper were in the middle of flower talk when we left. Chase and I dragged this one—" he pointed the knife in Logan's direction. "—outta there before he started interfering again."

The middle Jackson emerged from the fridge, triumphantly holding up four beers. "What? Just because I'm a guy, I can't have a say in the wedding?"

"Exactly that!" Chase exclaimed.

"Weddings are overrated," Eli mumbled to himself as he pulled forks out of the drawer. Neither one of us said anything about his remark because he had a really good reason for hating weddings.

Pushing off the frame, I moved to grab a plate. "What the hell happened there?" Next to me, Logan pointed at my hand. Funny how I felt the ache in my chest a lot more than the pain in my knuckles.

I lifted my shoulders and shoved a piece of pie into my mouth, "Nothing."

My friend eyed me suspiciously, but instead of voicing whatever was eating at him, he pulled his pie closer. There were a few moments of silence before our usual chatter resumed.

Eli told us about how his daughter, Molly, had taken to drawing and painting all of a sudden. But knowing the girl, it wouldn't be long before something else stole her attention. I had to hand it to Eli, he might've had his faults, but when it came to Molly, he'd do just about anything. And it showed. She wanted for nothing, especially not love.

"So," Logan drawled as we settled into our seats. After we'd made short work of the pie, we'd grabbed our beers and moved to the porch. "I think my little man has his first crush."

"Yeah?"

"Most definitely," I heard the amusement in Chase's voice.

Logan shook his head, a small smile playing on his lips. "The boy will not stop talking about Miss. Mazda and her super cool car."

Kenzie. Just thinking about her had my entire body tensing up. My throat closed and the beer that was making its way down became so thick, I choked on it.

My friends turned to me, concern etched on their faces as my coughing fit continued. "You okay man?" Logan asked. "You aren't pulling out Pop's tricks, are you?" Their father had a nasty habit of smoking in secret, much to his lungs' and their mother's dismay.

Nodding I pointed to my throat, "Wrong pipe."

"You need to teach that boy that most women are nothing more than a disappointment," Eli mused from his chair. He took a swig of his beer and relaxed even more into his seat, his eyes lingering on the trees surrounding the cabin. "Once they're done using you, they'll move on like you never even existed."

I couldn't agree more.

KENZIE

I STARED AT MY PHONE, DEBATING ON WHETHER TO SEND THE TEXT. It was late enough to be morning but still too early to be awake. *So why the hell can't I sleep?* "Ah, screw it," I mumbled and hit the *send* button. With a groan, I fell back and threw an arm over my eyes.

Damn you, Brett. Damn you to hell and back.

The phone I was still clutching buzzed to life, and I almost jumped off the bed. Breathing fast and hard, I checked the name flashing on the screen before pressing it to my ear. I barely had a chance to utter *hello* when Zoe's voice filtered through.

"Did I just read that right?" she huffed out. "You saw Brett?"

"I did." I closed my eyes at the memory.

"And you're staying at his girlfriend's guesthouse?"

"His girlfriend's grandma's guesthouse," I very pathetically corrected. After I opened my eyes, I pushed into a seated position. "Why are you up this early, anyway?"

"Just got home." Keys jangled in the background followed by the sound of a door closing. "Don't change the subject, Kenz. What happened?"

A host of unwanted emotions rushed through me, and I pressed the phone closer to my ear, "It was awful…" I told Zoe everything from the moment I saw Brett until his sudden departure. "Zoe, the anger radiated off him, which I don't get. I mean, if anyone has a right to be upset here, it's me."

"Sweetie, I don't know what to tell you," her voice sounded further away, and I figured she'd put me on speaker, "except, to close this chapter of your life you're going to need answers to those questions floating around in your head." When she spoke again, her voice was crystal clear. "I don't think you landed in Willow Creek by accident, Kenz."

I pulled my knees to my chest and wrapped my free arm around my legs. "I know."

"Listen, I've only got about five hours before I have to open the gallery." Zoe owned a very prestigious art gallery, and despite having amazing talent, she never displayed her own paintings. "Call me later?"

"Of course. Thanks for the call, Zoe."

"Anytime." I started to pull the phone away from my ear when I heard, "Oh and Kenz?"

"Yeah?"

"You're a lot stronger than you think."

The line went dead, and I stared into nothingness, hoping that my friend was right.

The Diner. The name was nothing if not practical. Bells above the door chimed when I stepped into the establishment. The sound of my heels clicking against the black-and-white checkered floor was almost deafening. I noticed an open spot by the counter and kept my eyes firmly fixed on the empty chair as I rushed forward.

I didn't have to look to know that most of the people were staring at me. I'd never felt as uncomfortable in my own skin as I did then. Sliding onto the stool, I was met with an "I'll be right with you." A woman with a thick auburn braid running down her back whooshed past me; coffee pot in hand.

"Hey there, stranger. What can I get you?"

I'd give just about anything for a vanilla latte, but I doubted it was on the menu. "Just a coffee, thanks."

"Comin' right up." She grabbed a mug from beneath the counter and filled it with my caffeine-fix before setting it down in front of me along with sugar and creamer. "I'm Lizzy, by the way." Her lips lifted into a warm, friendly smile. I returned her smile and introduced myself too. Leaning forward on her forearms, she asked, "Well, Kenzie, what brings you to our little town?"

Fate? Bad luck? "Car trouble," I added a bit more sugar than I usually took along with a whole heap of creamer and furiously stirred the concoction. Lizzy's expectant stare prompted me to add, "I was on my way to see a client in McKinney."

Nodding her head, she turned and busied herself with something I couldn't see. A few seconds later a slice of Pecan pie was placed in front of me. "It's never too early for pie," she suggested with a wink. "So, where were you drivin' from?"

I knew she was being hospitable, but her questions had me shifting in my seat. I dragged the pie closer and mumbled, "Uh, Texas City."

A low, drawn-out whistle blew over her lips. "That's a mighty long drive." She leaned closer. "The kind people take when they're running from something."

My brows pulled together, and I was on the verge of telling her to mind her own business when the bells chimed again. Whoever walked through the door brought a big smile to her lips.

She grabbed her coffee pot, and I swear she walked over to the newcomer with an extra sway in her hips.

I fiddled with the pie in front of me and gazed over to where Lizzy was chatting away with a very good looking man. The first words that came to mind were: *Tall, dark and handsome.* He did look a bit familiar though. While I tried to place where I'd seen this man before, the chiming alerted me to more newcomers.

The little diner was filling up by the second, and I desperately wanted to get out of there. I scanned the big board on the wall before I pulled a few notes from my purse and tucked them under the pie plate. Sliding off the stool, I kept my gaze firmly fixed on the door. I'd made it about halfway when the sound of someone hollering my name stopped me.

I turned to find little Flynn excitedly waving at me. The smile that graced my lips couldn't be helped; he was such a cute little boy. As I scanned over the adults behind him, I realized why the other man looked so familiar. Slap on a few tattoos, mess up his hair, give him a fuller beard, and he could easily pass as Logan. With the two men standing next to each other it was hard to miss the resemblance.

My gaze flitted to the door. *Would it be rude to just walk away?* When my focus returned to Flynn, I found three additional sets of eyes on me. Suppressing a heavy sigh, I headed over to the little boy and his family.

"Are you finding the guesthouse to your liking?" Logan asked after a quick *'hello'*. The assessing looks I received from most of the adults gave me the impression that they didn't care too much for me.

I straightened my spine and gave them the same smile I gave a client when I reassured them, I'd get them out of the PR mess they'd created for themselves. "It's perfect."

"My brother here seems to have forgotten his manners," the other man said as he pushed in front of Logan. "Chase."

I placed my hand in his outstretched one, and I'd bet the smile he gave me made a few women's hearts go pitter-patter. He also had an easy way about him that made me feel a little less uncomfortable. "Nice to meet you." I snatched my hand back and saw the woman tucked under Logan's arm looking at me with a small smile playing on her lips.

What is it with everyone constantly staring? Before I could voice my thought, little Flynn's whisper-shout sounded, "See mommy, I told you she was pretty."

My heart just about melted and I wondered what it would be like to have a family of my own. Normally I wouldn't allow myself the luxury of daydreaming. The last time I'd envisioned a possible future that included a husband and kids, my world had been knocked off its axis.

I shook off the thought and dropped, so I was eye-level with Flynn, "You're not so bad yourself." After I winked, I ruffled the boy's hair and straightened. Giving the dark-haired woman my attention, "You have an adorable son."

Her green eyes turned a shade brighter, and I saw nothing but motherly pride shine in them. Out of nowhere, a thought struck. *Did my mother look like that when she spoke about me or was her disapproval only reserved for me?* "He's pretty great," Flynn's mom's voice broke through the melancholy that had taken over.

I had no idea what the hell was going on with me, but I knew that I had to get out of there.

Out of the diner and out of that damn town.

"Any news on my car?" I aimed my clipped question at Logan.

He nodded tentatively and then explained, "You should be on your way in about three days." Pulling his lady closer, he continued, "Brett already ordered the parts we need."

I hated my heart for tightening at the sound of his name. After everything, it shouldn't react to him at all. Alas, that was not the case, as was proved at Sunday lunch. One look into those hazel depths had my pulse doing a fiery dance which was very inappropriate and unwelcome. And now I was stuck in his town for another three damn days. Maybe I should take advantage of those days and go find the answers that had been eluding me for years, to get closure.

"Since you're staying," Chase remarked. "You should come by Joe's later; it's ladies' night." He flashed his smile, and in my peripheral vision, I noticed Lizzy's gaze drop and a hint of sadness flash across her face.

"I—" the phone in my purse buzzed to life, and I gave Chase an apologetic look before pulling it out. After I saw Dean's name flash on the screen, I muted the thing. "I don't know." The last time I'd seen the inside of a bar was with Brett. I didn't go out drinking. Sure, Dean and I would have a glass of wine with dinner, and I'd have a glass of champagne at events, but that was it. Besides, my parents would have a heart attack if their daughter frequented bars and drank beer.

"Aw, come on?" Chase cocked his head, and his smile widened. "You're just gonna sit in your room and be lonely when you could spend the night with us." He threw his thumb over his shoulder, "I know he looks scary, but Harper has him on a tight leash."

"You should come," Lizzy insisted. "Us girls are always outnumbered, and Caleb makes the most delicious cocktails."

I had no idea what had gotten into me. Maybe there was something in the coffee, but I shocked myself when I answered, "I guess I could swing by for one drink."

"Yes," Lizzy exclaimed, her face lighting up. If I could borrow some of her excitement, I would be good.

'Goodbyes' and *'see you laters'* were said and when I stepped onto the sidewalk, I finally felt like I could breathe again. It was also the time I realized it wasn't the town or the people in it suffocating me; it was my own insecurities and unresolved past.

I planned to fix all of that, maybe then I could finally let go. But first I needed new clothes—business suits and high heels were not going to cut it in this town.

Chapter 7

BRETT

I WINCED.

Not because of the pain in my hand—which was a bit swollen and purple—but because of the crippling ache in my chest. Not being able to sleep, I'd made the mistake of going into the shop early. The sooner we got her car fixed, the sooner she could leave.

Unfortunately, even after a night of tossing and turning and trying to keep memories at bay, I wasn't prepared for the weight that settled inside me when I climbed into her car. As soon as I got a whiff of Kenzie's perfume still lingering in the air, I'd been bombarded with visions of the past.

"Holy hell, look at the legs on that one."

I turned from where I was trying to figure out what on earth I was looking at, to see what my friend Axil was on about. He'd been dragging me to these pop-up art galleries for weeks. Now, despite being an art student like me, he didn't attend them to get inspiration.

He only went to get laid.

I shook my head and followed his lusty gaze to two girls who were examining a painting called 'Sunburst.' Oranges and yellows formed abstract rays; it'd been one of my favorites of the day.

With her mini skirt barely covering her ass, I was certain Axil was referring to the blonde. However, it was the girl next to her that had me standing up straighter. Thick, caramel waves cascaded down her back. They looked so silky; my fingers immediately itched to touch.

"C'mon," Axil slapped me on the back before he started strutting toward the girls. Usually, I'd just leave him and be on my way. Not that day though. Without taking my eyes off the brunette, I started moving.

I'd never experienced such a pull before. It was like every cell in my body became more alive the closer I got to her. When we reached them, both girls turned around, and the breath got knocked right out of me. Eyes so blue, they just about saw through me, connected with mine and I was lost to whatever spell I was under.

I was vaguely aware of Axil using one of his pick-up lines on the blonde, but other than that, the whole world seemed to melt away. Discreetly, I wiped my palm on my jeans before holding out my hand. "Brett."

Her gaze dropped to the floor, and she pushed her hair behind her ear. When she looked up again, the shy smile playing on her lips had my heart doing funny things.

"Kenzie," she slipped her hand in mine and time completely stilled. Tiny pinpricks of electricity traveled up my arm and settled at the base of my skull. I wasn't unfamiliar with female company, but no other girl had me reacting the way I was responding to Kenzie.

Still holding her hand, I glanced over at Axil and the blonde flirting with each other. "You wanna get out of here?" I asked when I locked eyes with her again.

Hesitancy flashed over her features; I was sure she was going to turn me down. Her gaze flitted to her friend before returning to mine. "I'd love to."

Afraid she'd change her mind, I placed my hand on her back and led her toward the exit. Outside, the midday sun was almost blinding. With my cupped hand, I formed a shield above my eyes and scanned the immediate area.

"Where to now?" Kenzie's question drew my attention back to her. Man, she was gorgeous. I didn't know a thing about this girl, but that didn't stop me from wondering how her lips tasted or how her skin would feel beneath my fingertips.

I pointed to the small café across the street. "Coffee?"

Coffee turned into lunch which turned into dinner. I learned that Kenzie was a business major, at her father's behest, but she was still uncertain where her interests were. She loved blue butterflies, rainy days and sharing desserts. I discovered she had the most infectious laugh, and I wanted to hear a lot more of it. She also had this adorable thing where she'd avert her gaze and tuck her hair behind her ear whenever I complimented her. In a few short hours this girl had me falling for her so hard, I had no hopes of getting up again.

"I hate to break up your date, but it's closing time." I reluctantly tore my eyes away from Kenzie and found our waitress standing beside the table, bill in hand. That was the first time I noticed that the café was totally empty.

We apologized, paid our bill and headed out. The sun had made way for the moon, and still, I wasn't ready to let her go. I tugged her arm and pulled her to me. Swallowing hard, I *scanned her face. The way she was looking at me with those big, blue eyes made my chest ache. "I have to see you again."*

Kenzie curled her fingers around mine before she lifted onto her toes and pressed her lips to my cheek. I couldn't stop my lids from closing at the contact. When she pulled away, she pushed something into my palm and smiled sweetly. "Call me," she said before she turned and sauntered off.

Mouth agape I stared at the tiny piece of paper in my hand, and I knew without a doubt that this girl was going to change my life forever.

"Earth to Brett."

I blinked a couple of times and frowned when I saw Logan's face come into focus. "Ya know," he said. "Usually we fix the cars by working on their engines, not by sitting in them."

My frown deepened as I scanned my surroundings and realized I was still sitting in Kenzie's car. Feeling embarrassed, I shoved the door open and climbed out of the car hoping the memories would stay behind too. "Yeah, whatever," I muttered under my breath while I moved toward the front of the vehicle.

"So, we ran into Miss. Mazda at the diner," Logan declared. "She seems eager to get out of town."

I bet she does. There was no doubt in my mind that things between Kenzie and I needed to be resolved. For years and years, I'd wondered why she'd just abandoned me. No one knew this, but I'd gone looking for her a few years ago—what I found had me coming back to Willow Creek without so much as a backward glance.

"It's good to see at least one of you working." I had never been so happy to see Eli. I didn't want to hear about my friend's run-in with the woman I was desperately trying to forget. Eli let out a low whistle, "Nice wheels."

He wasn't wrong. The blood-red Mazda was low and sleek packed with features that any car aficionado would drool over. I didn't want to go there, but I bet Kenzie looked sexy as sin sitting behind the wheel, too.

I ground my teeth together and stifled a grunt.

Logan's chuckle brought me back to the present. "…maybe you should head over to Mrs. D's and show her some—" he waggled his brows, "—*southern hospitality*. Maybe it'll help remove the stick out of both y'alls asses."

It was a good thing that I wasn't holding a tool because the urge to fling it at my friend's head was strong as it was sudden.

Kenzie wasn't mine, and I had no right to want to hurl a tool at Eli too if he just thought about going over to the guesthouse.

And just like that, I was pissed at Kenzie again. How the hell did the woman still have that strong of a hold over me?

"Ha ha funny," Eli answered dryly. "I just came to drop off the pie momma sent, but now I'm thinking I'll just have it myself."

"Hey, hey, don't you dare leave this shop with my pie." Logan snatched the container from his brother and grinned. "You coming tonight?"

Eli flicked his wrist and pulled back the cuff of his shirt, "Yeah," he said when he dropped his arm again. "I'm dropping Molly off at about six."

"Flynn had his bag packed this morning already."

Eli made a weird sound that was probably meant to be a chuckle, "Molly threw all her drawing stuff in my truck, too. She's afraid I'll forget them. I'm not sure who's more excited over the Monday night sleepovers. The kids or the adults?"

"Oh, it's definitely the adults," Logan retorted.

There was no doubt that Logan and Harper adored their little boy, but I knew that my friend appreciated the one night a week he had his woman to himself for the entire night. I'd forgotten how it felt to spend a night just holding a woman. I tried to remember the last time I did and came up short. No one occupied that space in my heart after Kenzie. In my defense though, there was no heart to occupy. Kenzie had made sure of that, too.

The thoughts filled my chest with new bitterness. Again, I found myself envious of the people surrounding me. A heaviness settled on my chest. I was aware of Eli saying goodbye, but I only managed to grumble in return.

Logan had walked him out, and when I heard his footfalls draw near, I fiddled with a few parts under the hood under the guise of looking busy, willing my friend to go away.

"What's up with you?" Logan leaned his hip against the car and crossed his arms in front of his chest.

I fiddled some more. "Nothing."

My friend, unfortunately, was not deterred by my mood. "Ooh, somebody's panties are all twisted up."

Without giving him an answer, I moved to the workbench behind me and began tidying up the strewn about tools. I heard Logan chuckle before he slapped me on the back. "Or maybe you've lost your touch and had to settle for some self-love?"

The wrench I was holding dropped to the bench with a loud *clank*. Jaw clenching, I spun around and glared at him. "Back off, okay!"

"I told you—" hell-bent on saying what was on his mind, he ignored my anger and just spat out more words. "—at some point the women you're always entertaining are going to get tired of you just using them for a quick release."

"Dammit Logan," I yelled. "Just because you're stuck screwing the same woman every night doesn't mean I have to be."

Unmasked anger flashed on his face as he took a few determined steps toward me. "You watch your mouth," he seethed.

"Or what?" Clearly, I was past the point of reasoning because I would never intentionally bate my friend for a fight.

Logan gave me a two-second-death-stare. "Or I ram my fist through it."

"Yeah, I'd like to see you try."

We were about a second away from settling things like a pair of adolescent boys when Harper's loud, "Hey," reverberated through the shop. I blinked, and she was standing between us with her hand pressed against Logan's chest. When she looked at me, I swear I saw understanding shine in her eyes. "I think you need to take a walk."

She wasn't wrong, I needed to clear my head. I gave her a small nod and turned for the door. As I walked away, I heard her ask Logan, "What happened?"

"He was being an idiot."

There were a few seconds of silence during which I felt their eyes on me before Harper continued in that soft voice that she only reserves for the men in her life. "Or maybe he is hurting and lashing out is his way of dealing with it."

Her assessment was so accurate it had me speeding up and storming out of the shop. Blinded by anger and whatever else was brewing inside me, I stomped down the sidewalk utterly oblivious to the pedestrians until it was too late.

KENZIE

"OH, I'M—" I BENT DOWN AND PICKED UP MY SHOPPING that had slipped from my hands when I'd walked into someone. After I retrieved the fallen items, I pushed to my feet and looked straight at Brett. At his bobbing Adam's apple to be precise. "—sorry." The single word blew over my lips in a whisper.

I didn't want to, but I knew not making eye contact was cowardly, so ever so slowly my gaze traveled from his neck, over his now fuller beard and settled on his rich hazel eyes. There was so much intensity burning behind them; for a split second the past just melted away, and we were just two people standing in front of each other.

"You okay?" His voice sounded both strained and clipped.

Nodding, I was grateful for having both hands occupied; the sudden need to fiddle with my hair was almost unbearable. Brett shoved his hands into the front pockets of his Levi's; both of us seemingly unable to move.

"Your car should be ready in a few days."

Although we were standing outside, it felt as if we'd been dropped into a tiny room with all the air sucked out. I could barely breathe with him standing so close. Conflicting emotions scrambled up my already confused thoughts.

My pulse started its fiery dance again, and the usually dormant butterflies in my tummy joined in. I had to admit it was a little disconcerting that I still reacted to this man the same way I had the first time I'd seen him.

"I know," I finally managed. "Logan already told me."

He opened his mouth to say something but shut it again as if he thought better of the idea. This was weird. I couldn't even imagine how strange it looked to the people who sidestepped us. Honestly, how could two people standing in the middle of a sidewalk, staring at each other not seem odd?

"How have you been?" It was probably the lamest thing I could ask, but unfortunately, that was all my brain offered up.

Confusion drew Brett's brows together, but it didn't stop him from saying. "Good. You?"

My tongue slid over my lips, and I noticed his gaze drop to my mouth for a second before he snapped it away and the muscle in his jaw started to jump. "Uh… good."

Gosh, this was beyond awkward. The longer I stood there, the more constricted my airway felt. I swallowed hard, to relieve some of the pressure. It didn't help.

But even with all the awkwardness swallowing us up, I wasn't ready for us to part ways. "I always figured when I ran into you again, it would be at some fancy art studio or something."

"Yeah, well—" his voice had an icy edge to it. "—life didn't work out as planned." I heard the accusation, and I felt its pressure like an anvil dropped on my chest.

"Speaking of life plans," he went on. "You working for your daddy's company?"

I tightened my grip on the shopping bags. Brett had been the only person who I ever confided in about the reservations I had over working for my father. Even back then I had no idea what I'd wanted to do with my life; my future in business had been decided before I'd even taken my first breath.

Then life threw me a bone in the form of a six-foot-three sexy-as-sin art student. He'd showed me that it was okay not to know where you were headed and it was even better to dream of where you wanted to be.

For a while back then, I'd been drawing strength from the way being with Brett had made me feel. I'd begun to believe that I could spread my wings and fly where *I* wanted to fly. Then he went away and sent me that horrible letter, and just like that my wings had been clipped and I was destined to never fly again.

I made sure to keep the sadness out of my voice when I answered, "Yes, I am his CEO."

The muscle in his jaw started ticking faster, and his eyes turned deathly cold. "Of course you are."

"What's that supposed to mean?"

Brett shook his head and took a step backward. "Once a daddy's girl, always a daddy's girl, right?" Another step backward. "Did you actually have to work for that position or did dear old dad just hand it to you for being his obedient lap dog?" The vein in his neck ticked and nothing but hatred flashed in his eyes. "I can't bloody do this." One more step back. "I can't stand here and make niceties with *you*."

Anger raged through my veins. "You're an asshole," I dropped the bags and stomped forward. "You keep running away like you're nursing some gaping wound," I realized I was verging on the edge of sounding hysterical, I didn't care. "Newsflash, Brett, you were the one who hurt *me* with your terrible insults. I've apologized to you! I can't change the damn past! And it's not my fault that you are stuck on sulk-mode."

His face morphed into something unrecognizable. I held my stance as he headed straight for me, I didn't even blink when we were toe-to-toe, and his head dropped, so we were at eye-level.

"Every single word in that letter was deserved," each word he spat at me dripped acid. The anger and hurt I saw burning in his eyes lit a flame in my soul. "You think I'm sulking? After everything you put me through, you're the one standing here crying over a letter. What about me, Kenzie? I gave you everything I had to give and still it wasn't enough."

Brett closed his eyes briefly, and after he opened them again, he took a deep inhalation and straightened. "If I'm an asshole, then it's you who turned me into one."

A mixture of guilt, anger, and sadness had tears stinging the back of my eyes while I watched him stalk off. I'd always been so hung up on how he'd left me that I'd conveniently forgotten that this man gave up his freedom for me.

I focused on the cold look in his eyes while I dropped to my haunches to gather up the bags I'd thrown down. I needed to remember that icy gaze the next time I conjured up fantasies about Brett Carter.

BRETT

I SUCKED IN A DEEP BREATH WHILE I STARED AT THE ENTRANCE TO JOE'S. Not only were Monday nights ladies' night, but it was also the only night during the week all six of us got together for a drink. When I'd first moved to Willow Creek, it had been just Logan and me. We'd quickly learned that ladies' nights were the best nights to pick up women who were just looking to have a good time.

Not long after, Chase started to join us. Eli only ever joined us for a drink. In all the time I'd known him I had never seen that guy leave with a woman.

Logan started showing up less and less shortly after Harper had moved to town; he'd spent all his nights pining after her until he finally broke through all her walls. With little Flynn thrown into the mix, nights out were in short supply. Since the girls could drink for half the price on Mondays, it kind of just made sense that we chose that day to all hang out together. Eli's daughter, Molly, and Flynn usually spent the night with Logan's parents, which gave the adults the chance to let loose for a bit.

Not that Logan and Harper took the opportunity to drink; they usually left after about two rounds. It didn't take a genius to figure out what they were up to.

That thought brought my mind straight back to another person.

The exchange between Kenzie and me had weighed heavy on me for the remainder of the day. I couldn't even blink without seeing the hurt in her eyes or feeling my own anger bubble through my veins. That girl—no, she was all woman now—twisted my wires in the worst way. One moment I wanted to never see her again and in the next I needed to take all her pain away.

What the hell is wrong with me?

Tonight, more than ever, I needed the comfort my circle of friends provided. Even though Logan and I had shared some words earlier that day, I knew that my friends would still welcome me to the table without hesitancy.

That's what family did.

Raking a hand through my hair, I tugged at the door with the other. As expected, the place was packed. Our local haunt might've been named Joe's, but it was not owned by a *Joe*. Well, not anymore. Caleb, the current owner, had inherited the place from his uncle and didn't bother with changing the name.

My eyes did a lazy sweep across the crowded room. To a stranger, this place would look sketchy and run-down. The off-white floors sported more than a few scuff marks, and the lightwood bar that ran the length of the building needed a good polishing. Bullhorns along with rodeo pictures adorned the open-faced brick walls.

Yeah, this place didn't look it, but it certainly was one of the best places to take a load off.

I spotted my friends gathered around one of the tables next to the old jukebox. Before I headed to them, I made my way to the bar, ducking behind a customer when I caught sight of Lola serving a patron. The action was nothing less than cowardly; I just didn't have the strength to face her now—even though she might be exactly what I needed to get my mind off of Kenzie.

When she moved to the other end of the bar, I slipped to the side and patiently waited for Caleb to serve me.

"The usual?" He asked while he pushed a red wine toward the woman standing next to me.

"Yeah and tequila for the table," I jerked my head in the direction of my friends.

"Comin' right up." When Caleb moved to fix my drink order, I turned around. With my elbows resting on the wooden surface behind me, I scanned the crowd, my gaze landed on the table next to the jukebox.

As usual, Logan and Harper were huddled as close together as they could get; his arm protectively draped over her shoulders. Behind his beer, Eli was brooding, and it looked like he wanted to be anywhere but there. Chase was stealing glances at Lizzy who was surveying the crowd—possibly looking for her next roll in the hay.

I shook my head and silently chuckled to myself. I couldn't wait for those two to finally realize what the rest of us had known for years.

"Look what the cat dragged in."

At the sound of Lola's voice, the smile slipped from my lips. Slowly, I slid my arms off the bar and turned around. With her hand planted on her jutted out hip, she gave me a glare that told me she was not impressed with me one bit.

"Meeting up with the gang," I remarked.

Her gaze traveled to my friends' table, and for a minute I thought I saw longing flash over her features. With a knitted brow she looked at me again. Tapping the bar twice, she mumbled, "You have fun now," before she moved away to help a newcomer.

"Hey, Lo!"

The hopeful look in her eyes when she glanced over her shoulder just cemented my decision. I heard Logan's words ring in my ears loud and clear. *'I know this thing with her is casual for you, but does she see it that way?'* I need to man-up and end whatever this was.

She fluttered her lashes, "Yeah?"

"You and me—" I waved my finger between us, "—need to talk later."

Lola sauntered back to me, "Later as in at your cabin later, mmm?"

I shook my head, "No, as in before I leave."

For a second I thought I saw sadness flit across her face, but it was gone so soon it might've been my imagination. "I'll come find you when I have a few minutes to spare."

I was still figuring out where I'd crossed the line with Lola when Caleb placed my order in front of me.

"Are ya startin' a tab?"

I grabbed my beer and slid the tray of shots from the counter and nodded, "Yeah." Reaching the table without spilling the contents in my hands took some maneuvering on my part. When I placed the shots in the center of the table, everyone except Logan seemed happy to see me.

Eyes narrowed, we stared at each other. I lifted one shoulder in a small shrug, and a smile stretched across my friend's face.

He pushed to his feet and feigned a punch to my shoulder before he said, "No hard feelings, man."

That there was my relationship with my best friend. We fought like family, and we made up like it too.

I pulled a chair out and lowered my tired body onto it. Taking a long swallow of the beer, I finally felt the tension slowly seep out of my pores. To my left, I noticed that Eli seemed a bit more…*off* than he usually was. I knew better than to ask him about it though.

"What happened to your hand?"

Harper's question earned me the attention of everyone else around the table. I looked down at my bruised knuckles; opening and closing my fist to test the pain. It still hurt but not nearly as much as the gaping hole in my chest ached.

"I, uh, banged it up while pulling an engine." I felt the weight of Logan's stare at my lie. We hadn't needed to pull an engine in quite some time. Lucky for me, my friend didn't say a word.

"You have to keep icing it to keep the swelling down," Harper's voice was filled with concern. "Are you taking something for the pain?" She gave me a pointed stare, "You can't mix alcohol and medication."

Logan tugged her closer and kissed the top of her head. "Sugar, he is a grown-ass man, let him be."

She leveled him with a stare too before a smile broke free. With a quick lift of her shoulders, she insisted, "It's not my fault you lot need constant mothering."

"I'll drink to that." Lizzy lifted her glass in the air before she brought it to her lips. "By the way," she eyed me over the rim of her glass. "I heard you and the new girl—" she set her glass down and tapped her chin. "—Hmm, how do I put this?" I held my breath while she stared at the ceiling pretending to think. The last thing I needed was the town gossiping about Kenzie and me getting into a screaming match.

"Had an altercation," Lizzy exclaimed, triumphantly pointing at me.

"You been at the hair salon again, Liz?" Logan asked. "You know those old ladies love to gossip about nothing. Remember how the entire town thought Harper and I were getting married after only one date? I'll give you a guess where the rumor started."

Laughter erupted around the table, and I gave a nod of thanks to my friend, who still had my back after our little tiff.

Lizzy proceeded to explain to us, in a very animated way, how Mrs. Atwood described to her what she apparently saw. Much to my relief, everyone just shrugged it off, and soon the conversation drifted to how Eli had treated Harper when she arrived.

The laughter around the table got louder as we downed our shots and ordered a few more. My gaze flitted from one happy face to the next, and all I could do was shake my head and guzzle down another swig of beer. I'd often wondered how my life would've ended up if I hadn't had these people to keep me sane.

"Have you made a decision about that property yet?" Chase directed his question at Eli. The property in question was an old farmhouse that was going to require a lot of work, but what made it really alluring was the fact that it was next to his parents' ranch.

"Yeah," answered Eli. "I think it will be best for Molly if Mom and Pop are close by, ya know."

Harper laughed, "Flynn is going to be so excited." The house Harper and Logan were in the middle of renovating were just down the road from the property Eli was interested in. I grinned to myself as I imagined all the Jackson boys buying up the property surrounding their parents. We'd have to rename the creek to Jackson Creek.

"I hope you boys are ready to work," this coming from Eli. "The main house is livable but there is a small cottage adjacent to the house, and I'm thinking of turning it into a playhouse for Molly."

The only time you'd ever see any kind of emotion coming from Sheriff Jackson was when he spoke about his daughter. His normally cold eyes would light up, and his lips would twitch from the smile just wanting to break free.

"Maybe I can finally convince you to adopt one of the animals?" Chase sounded hopeful.

Eli shook his dark head and took another swig of beer. "Getting an animal is a huge responsibility. I think I'll wait till Molly is a bit older."

"She's seven," Logan stated. "That girl is more grown-up than actual grownups. I think she'll be able to handle a pet."

"We'll see."

"Wow!" Lizzy exclaimed. "She cleans up good."

I, along with the rest of my friends, followed her gaze to the entrance of Joe's. My lungs collapsed in one fell swoop as I watched Kenzie nervously enter the bar.

She'd swapped her stifling business suit and heels for a pair of Levi's that might as well have been painted onto her, and a tank top that was definitely going to draw everyone's attention to her chest. Her hair tumbled over her shoulders and paired with the brown leather cowboy boots on her feet; she looked good.

Way too damn good.

"I take it that is the owner of the Mazda?" I barely heard Eli's question through the *whooshing* in my ears.

Without being able to stop it, my mouth opened, and words came rushing out. "Kenzie Michaels. Her daddy owns Renowned

Eminence. Whenever politicians and celebrities want something swept under the rug, they go to Walter Michaels."

"And you know this how?" Chase asked.

Ignoring his question, I brought my beer to my lips, still unable to take my eyes off Kenzie as she weaved through the crowd. She turned to the side to dodge a guy with an arm full of drinks and my gaze zeroed in on her ass.

The yeasted drink that slid down my throat did nothing to alleviate the sudden dryness I felt. The intricate *K* that sat just above my heart singed me straight to my core; I had to keep myself from reaching up and rubbing the tender spot.

"Well, seeing as I'm the one who invited her, I'll escort her to our table." Chase jumped from his chair. Before I could really register what he was doing, let alone stop him, he was already halfway to Kenzie. A feeling, I refused to acknowledge as jealousy, burned its way through my veins as I watched him sidle in beside her.

My eyes narrowed while I meticulously took in the exchange between them. Chase explained something and pointed toward our table. Kenzie followed his outstretched hand and our gazes locked. Even from where I sat, I saw her little gasp.

She turned her attention back to Chase and shook her head. He leaned in closer and gave her a smile I knew he used to get women in bed. I gritted my teeth and fought against the sudden need to strangle my best friend's brother.

With more force than was necessary, I plonked my beer down. Paying no attention to my friends' confused stares; I pushed to my feet and stalked toward the bathroom. As much as I wanted to punch something, I resisted the urge and splashed some cold water on my face.

"You wanna talk about it?"

When I looked up, Logan was leaning against the wall next to the door. I threw my head back and focused on the flashing light above me. What I wanted was to be in control of my emotions; to not give a shit if someone was coming on to Kenzie. If she'd pack up and vacate the space she occupied in my heart, that would be great too.

I dragged my hand over my face and released a breath.

"She's the one, isn't she?" His tone told me he'd wait all night for my answer. "The reason you were in jail?" I'd met Logan while we were both doing time. He was doing a three-year stint for drunk driving and I was rotting away for a crime I didn't commit.

"Yeah." I croaked out. "I haven't seen her in twelve years." That wasn't the truth. A few years ago, I'd looked her up. I thought if she was still so ingrained in me after all those years that maybe, *maybe*, I also held a place in her heart.

I'd gone to Texas City with the intention of getting her back, and I found her in another man's arms. Knowing that she could move on while I stayed stuck in the past stung in the worst possible way, and even though I wanted to, I still couldn't muster up an ounce of hate toward her.

Anger. Now *that* I had in spades.

"Walter would have killed her if he found out she was using, hell, I didn't even know until that night," I lifted my shoulders in a shrug. "I took the blame, never once thinking that she'd just leave me like that."

"I get it, man. We'll do just about anything to protect the ones we love." He sounded wistful, and I knew he was thinking about the time Harper's ex had kidnapped her and little Flynn. Logan hadn't given up on finding his family, not even when Eli refused to help.

"I also know—" he continued "—that love that strong only comes around once in a lifetime and it has the ability to completely obliterate us." He pushed off the wall and stalked toward me. "But if we let it in, it can be the most beautiful thing."

I opened my mouth, and he cut in again, "Oh, and Chase is only flirting with her to make Lizzy jealous. One of these days I'm going to lock them in a room until they admit their feelings." My brows drew together, and Logan laughed heartily. "Don't think I didn't see ya staring daggers at my little brother."

Embarrassed that I'd been caught, I shook my head. "Whatever, man." I moved toward the exit. "And why the hell are we yapping in the bathroom like a couple of girls?"

My ass-hat friend laughed even louder. I pulled on the door and immediately stopped short when our table came into view. "Aw, hell no."

KENZIE

I FOLLOWED CHASE AS HE MOVED THROUGH THE FROLICKING PATRONS TOWARD HIS FRIENDS. He'd been relentless, and when I saw that Brett wasn't sitting at the table anymore, I agreed to join them for a couple of drinks. The truth was I'd welcome just about any distraction to keep my mind off of Brett. Bringing my hand up, I toyed with the butterfly pendant around my neck, willing my racing heart to slow down.

The seriousness held in Brett's eyes had affected me, even from across a crowded room. No other man had that effect on me, and I suspected no other man ever would. When we reached the table, Chase pulled out a chair. After I sat down, he placed my wine in front of me. I had to remind myself that it was in bad taste to gulp everything down in one go.

Instead, I dragged the glass closer to me and toyed with the stem.

"Glad you could make it." I recognized the woman as Flynn's mom. "I never did get to introduce myself this morning before Chase here forgot *his* manners." The smile she aimed at him held no contempt. "I'm Harper." She jerked her head to the side. "You already know Chase and Lizzy, and that guy—" she pointed to the man a chair away from me. He looked a lot like Logan and Chase, only he had a brooding, intimidating look about him. "—is Eli."

Eli aimed his beer at me before he took a swig. "He also happens to be the Sheriff," I heard Lizzy say. She shared a look with Harper that I had no hope of understanding. I probably looked like an idiot, just staring at all of them with an uncomfortable look on my face. If Zoe were there, she'd have known exactly what to say to get rid of all the awkwardness.

"What brings you to our town?" Eli's deep voice broke through the silence.

"Oh, her car broke down," Lizzy answered for me, which earned her a look equivalent to one a disobedient student would get from a headmaster. *Geez, he's intense.*

"I wasn't asking you, Lizzy."

The redhead sliced her hand through the air and huffed, "Haven't you learned by now that your tone doesn't work on me, *Sheriff.*"

Chase let out a hearty laugh while Harper hid her amusement behind her glass. Oddly, that had me feeling a little more comfortable.

However, as soon as my shoulders relaxed, the sheriff's eyes traveled back to me, his glare holding a lot of distrust. I brought my wine to my lips and took a big gulp. Movement sounded next to me, and when I looked over, Eli's stare had been replaced by Brett's.

Out of the corner of my eye, I caught sight of Logan taking a seat next to Harper. It was possible that he greeted me, but I couldn't be sure because my attention was held hostage by Brett.

He didn't look too pleased to see me, but he did look insanely hot. I chided myself for noticing. I shouldn't be thinking about what lay beneath that tightly stretched white tee or wondering if he still had that tattoo on his chest. My fingers shouldn't itch to touch his skin, and my tongue shouldn't want to know the taste of him.

Yet, that's exactly what I wanted.

Heat crept up my cheeks at the direction of my thoughts. I pushed my hair behind my ear, and just before I averted my gaze, his forehead creased. Inside my pocket, my cell buzzed, sending my already racing heart on an even wilder gallop. I excused myself and moved to the back of the bar where the music wasn't as loud.

I made the mistake of answering without looking at the caller ID, "Hello?"

"Kenzie? It's me, can you hear me?"

Dean's voice carried through the line and with it came a tidal wave of guilt. "I hear you."

"What's going on? I've been calling you, I don't even know how many times, and you haven't—" there was a slight pause and then, "—is that music I hear? Kenzie, where are you?"

The sternness in his voice reminded me of my dad, and for whatever reason, it ticked me off. "I'm having a drink at a bar, Dean."

"You're where?" he sounded incredulous.

I had no desire to explain myself. "My phone's about to die, I'll call you in the morning." I didn't wait for his reply; after stabbing the little red button, I powered down my phone. My gaze dropped to the lifeless device in my palm, and I glared at it as if it was the cause of all my problems.

After I shoved the thing back into my pocket, I began walking back to the table, only to be rooted to the spot by a pair of hazel eyes that seared me to the very bottom of my soul.

I couldn't move. Hell, I could barely breathe when he looked at me like that. Brett pushed to his feet, I held my breath. As we stood like that, staring at each other, the sounds that filled the room slowly fell away. Was I a bad person for wanting him the way I did? Was it wrong to wish that, for one night only, the past didn't exist?

He took a step forward, my teeth dug into my lower lip.

He took another step, then another and another. The closer he got, the louder my heart drummed. Common sense told me I should be moving too; meet him halfway, run in the opposite direction…anything really. I just couldn't. Cinder blocks sat where my boots used to be.

He stopped in front of me, and all the air in my lungs was replaced with his manly scent. I had to stop myself from closing my eyes and inhaling his earthy smell more deeply.

His eyes traveled the length of me in a slow perusal. After the words we'd had earlier that day, I wondered if it was judgment or appreciation I saw in his eyes.

"Kenzie," The way my name rolled off his tongue when our gazes collided again had my whole body vibrating. "Can—"

"Brett! I'm ready for that *conversation* now!" In a second Lola was standing between Brett and me, both of her hands flattened against his chest. She gave me a quick glance over her shoulder before turning her attention back to him. "That is if you're not busy."

His gaze stayed pinned on me, so many emotions swirling in the depth of his eyes. I saw pain, sadness, and heat. No, that couldn't be right. How could a man that had no regard for me look at me with want in his eyes?

"Brett?" Lola's voice was filled with irritation.

I took that as my cue to leave. Stepping around the pair, I made my way back to the table. This time I didn't care about good manners, I reached for my glass and didn't stop swallowing until it was empty.

"Thirsty?" Chase asked.

I nodded, "Very."

With a chuckle, he grabbed my glass and suggested, "Let me get you a refill."

My gaze skittered to where I'd left Lola and Brett a moment ago. I caught them just in time to see him lead her away with his hand on her elbow. I grabbed Chase by the wrist, "Can you get me something stronger than wine, please?"

After a quick nod, he made his way to the bar while I was met with a few inquisitive glances from the others and a dead-on stare from Eli. Giving him a glare of my own, I hissed, "I'll be home by ten, and I promise not to drink and drive, Sheriff."

Both Lizzy and Harper did their best to hide their smiles whereas Logan threw his head back and laughed. Eli grunted something as he stood and headed toward Chase.

"You're not so bad, Miss. Mazda," this coming from Logan.

For the first time since I'd arrived in Willow Creek, I felt some of the tension leave my body. "Thanks, I guess?"

Lizzy scooted over and took the empty chair next to me, "So, you were on your way to see a client right?" When I nodded, she continued, "What is it that you do exactly?"

Usually, when people asked Zoe this question, her eyes would dance with happiness while she described the gallery and her love for art. I knew mine wouldn't. "The short answer: when a client needs to change the way the public views them, we step in and find a way to shine a positive light on them."

She seemed thoughtful for a moment. "What you're saying is, if—hypothetically speaking—the president was your client and he'd been caught with his fingers in the secretary's cookie jar, you'd step in and make it go away?"

"Sort of. We don't make it go away. There really is no such thing as bad publicity. We just make sure that the good outweighs the bad. For instance, in this hypothetical case, I'd arrange for the president to help out at soup kitchens or visit the children's ward…you know, things that tug at heartstrings and make him seem like a really great guy who only made one little mistake."

"Wow, that sounds interesting." Lizzy sounded as underwhelmed as I felt. After I'd introduced Brett to my parents for the first time, my dad had made no secret of the fact that he didn't like him. He'd cautioned that a boy like that would only drag me down and probably break my heart in the process. When it'd turned out that Dad was right about the last part, I'd stopped fighting them and figured that they knew what was best for me.

So, I ended up in a job that I didn't love.

Looking back, I didn't even know what came over me when I murmured, "It's not really. Most days I deal with insufferable, self-centered people who only care about themselves."

"Doesn't sound like you enjoy your job?" Harper remarked.

Where is Chase with that damn drink? "I don't." *And why am I being this transparent?* My skin started to itch as uneasiness pulled my muscles together. Besides Zoe, I'd never admitted to a single soul that I didn't like my job. And if anyone would ask me what my dream job would be, I wouldn't have an answer. The thing was; I hadn't made a decision for myself in years.

"You know," Harper's soft voice broke through the loudness of my thoughts. "You shouldn't be where you're unhappy. It will steal too much from you." There was a myriad of emotion in her voice, and when Logan's fingers brushed over her cheek, I knew there was a story there.

I sensed Brett's presence at the same time as a colorful drink was placed in front of me. Ignoring the strong pull to my left, I looked to my right and asked, "What's this?"

Chase waggled his brows and grinned, "Tequila Sunrise." He turned his attention to Lizzy, "You're in my seat."

She rolled her eyes and made a big show of inspecting the chair. "Funny, I don't see your name on it anywhere."

Laughing to myself, I turned my attention to my drink; the name was fitting. Out of nowhere, my mind drifted to the first time I'd met Brett. I'd been looking at a painting that had similar colors. I chanced a look to my left, and sure enough, those beautiful, intense eyes of his were still focused on me.

I wanted to yell: *If you hate me so much, why are you looking at me like I'm something you want?* Instead, I wrapped my lips around the straw and sucked down a good amount of my drink. This was dangerous, it tasted fruity and sweet, and I immediately went back for more.

Chatter had started up around the table. Harper and Lizzy were discussing where she could find a wedding dress, as Willow Creek had just about every kind of shop except a bridal boutique. Logan and Chase were in the middle of a heated discussion over which bike engine was the strongest. The bits of their conversation I heard sounded like Greek to me, so I just tuned them out. Brett and Eli didn't talk as much as grunt now and then when they didn't agree with something.

As I looked around the table, I found myself jealous of the connection these people had. Sure, I had Zoe, and I loved her like a sister, but she was all I had. My parents and even Dean didn't know who I really was underneath the business suits and pulled back hair. I couldn't really blame Dean for not knowing though. I'd made absolutely no effort to be anything less than what was expected of me.

"What do *you* think, Kenzie?"

At the sound of my name, I snapped back to reality and Lizzy's expectant gaze on me.

"Sorry, what?" I heard a slight whoosh in my ears, and my cheeks suddenly felt warm. Wanting to ease the dryness in my throat, I pulled my drink closer only to find it was empty. *I can't even remember drinking the entire thing.*

"I said Harper and I should take a trip down to Texas City, she'll definitely find a dress there."

"Yeah, for sure." I pushed to my feet to go get another drink but sat back down once Lola appeared with an entire tray of them. She aimed a smile at Brett before placing another Tequila Sunrise in front of me.

"Thank you," Eagerly, I pulled the drink closer.

"Enjoy." Her voice had an odd tone to it, but I ignored it just as I overlooked the fact that my drink tasted a bit stronger this time around.

The more alcoholic fruitiness I consumed, the less tense I felt, and that was all I cared about.

BRETT

"THERE WAS A TIME WHEN I USED TO LOOK AT HARPER LIKE THAT, and I distinctly remember you giving me shit for it."

I didn't have to look to know that Logan was wearing a way-too-smug grin on his face. "If memory serves, you told me to piss off."

A hearty laugh filled the air before his palm connected with my back. "Why don't you just go talk to her instead of ogling her like a pervert?"

That was an excellent question, I thought to myself while I toyed with the label on the beer bottle. After Eli and Chase had called it a night, over an hour ago, I'd moved to the bar with the intent of heading home. I could get the same buzz there without having to look at Kenzie the whole damn time. Having her so close to me filled my mind with visions I didn't want there.

Her body pressed against mine; my fingers tangled in her hair, my lips on her skin, my—

I clenched my jaw in irritation. This was her fault. Why did she have to come to my town looking all sorts of sexy when my heart hadn't even begun to recover?

"Brett?" Logan's voice interrupted my musings. The slight edge to his tone had me wondering if he'd been talking to me for a while.

With a lot of effort, I tore my eyes away from where Kenzie was chatting with Harper and Lizzy. "What?"

The smug bastard laughed again before he shook his head, "There is no hope for you, man. No hope." His shaking shoulders disappeared into the crowd, and even though I knew he couldn't see it, I still glared at him.

My gaze flitted back to the girls just in time to see Lizzy select a new song on the jukebox. A familiar rock-and-roll tune filtered through the wall mounted speakers, and I just hoped Kenzie would keep her ass planted on the chair.

The last time I'd seen her move, we hadn't even made it home before I'd had her out of her clothes and under me—or rather on top of me...in the front seat of my car. My lips twitched at the memory.

Kenzie pushed to her feet, I swallowed hard. A smile filled with pure happiness or maybe alcohol spread across her lips, and she nodded furiously. *Oh, boy.* It started out as a subtle sway of her hips as she made her way to Lizzy and Harper. The three women formed a little circle, and the hip-swaying kicked up a notch.

I couldn't tear my eyes off of Kenzie even if I tried. Both her arms reached for the sky while her swaying hips looked more sensual by the minute. Transferring my weight from one foot to the other, I swallowed down what was left of my drink.

Images of us moving like that together flashed in my mind. I imagined sliding in behind her and splaying my fingers across her abdomen, pressing her back to my front. Not even space for a breath between us. My hand on her hip and my mouth nipping at her neck. I could already hear the needy moans blowing over her lips.

I licked my lips and…something was wrong. Kenzie wobbled and spread her arms wide, like someone trying to regain their balance. Lizzy grabbed one of her arms and said something to which Kenzie shook her head. The concerned look on Lizzy and Harper's faces caused me to stand up straighter.

Harper motioned to Logan who was seated at the table, he pushed to his feet. I frowned, I hadn't meant to, but I'd kept track of Kenzie's drinks. I could be wrong, but I didn't think three drinks were enough to render someone drunk. And yet as she stumbled off to the ladies, she looked exactly that.

"Looks like the city girl can't handle her drink." The cheeriness in Lola's tone gave me pause. We'd had a misunderstanding earlier in the evening when I'd told her that I didn't think we should sleep together anymore. I was afraid that Logan was right and that she'd eventually want more. I didn't have anything to offer a woman.

The *'No Vacancy'* sign above my heart was lit up in bright flashing lights.

She didn't seem like the petty kind, but then again, the only thing I knew about her was how she looked without clothes. Lizzy came to Kenzie's side, and once they disappeared into the bathroom, I turned to Lola.

"What did you do?"

"Me?" She batted her eyelashes in a very over the top way. "I simply showed her some Southern hospitality."

I clenched my jaw so tight, pain shot to my ears. Instead of fantasizing about all the things I'd wanted to do to Kenzie, I should've noticed something was off when Lola kept bringing drinks. Biting my tongue, I gave the woman in front of me a hard stare when what I really wanted to do was shake her and ask what the hell was wrong with her.

Angry with myself and disappointed in Lola, I pushed off the bar and headed to the back. Logan already stood beside the ladies' room door. "Harper in there, too?" I propped my shoulder against the wall.

He nodded, "The girls are tending to her, she doesn't look too good, man."

My glare automatically snapped to Lola who was serving a customer. "Lola's been spiking her drinks," I aimed my stare at Logan. "And before you say *I told you so'* or some shit like that, I'm telling you, now is not the time."

Logan shook his head, "What can we do?"

A sigh blew over my lips, and I squeezed my eyes shut. When I opened them again, the door was my sole focus. "I'm not taking her to the guesthouse tonight. She can sleep it off at my place."

"You sure?"

It probably wasn't the best idea, but it didn't matter how angry I was with Kenzie, there was no way I would leave her in that state by herself. "Positive."

A minute later, the women emerged; Kenzie looked a little worse for wear. Her skin was pale and her long strands stuck to her cheeks. I stepped forward and took over for Lizzy and Harper who were holding her upright.

I threw her limp arm over my shoulder and wrapped mine around her waist. "Wh-what are you doing?" she mumbled.

"I'm taking ya home."

Kenzie tried to pull away from me but ended up stumbling forward; I caught her with my other arm and pulled her to my chest. I had to take a steadying breath; I wasn't prepared for how good it would feel to hold her again. But that wasn't the place nor the time to be reveling in the feel of all her softness pressed against me. Her head lolled back, and a lazy smile spread across her face. "Oh! Hi, Brett." She accentuated the last letters of my name and then giggled to herself. Man, she was so freaking out of it.

"Can you walk?"

She didn't answer me. Instead, she curled her fingers around my biceps and squeezed. "Have you been working out?" The question slurred from her lips. "Your muscles are so huge and so hard." Another giggle fit erupted from her. I turned my attention to the ceiling, and after I let out a long, slow breath, I bent down and hauled Kenzie into my arms.

"She only had like three cocktails." Lizzy mused.

Kenzie mumbled something and snuggled into my neck. Big, loud warning bells rang in my ears. *This is a stupid idea.* I locked eyes with my friend and found the same concern etched on his face.

Cocking his head to the side, Logan asked, "You good?"

"Yeah." A lie, of course. Hiking Kenzie higher in my arms, I headed for the exit.

I caught sight of Lola watching us as I walked out of Joe's with my friends close behind me. A string of curses fell from my lips, but to my surprise, no one uttered a word. My emotions were all over the place as we put her in my truck and I headed toward my cabin. The anger that'd wrapped itself around my heart for so many years slowly made way for… I didn't even know what. All I knew was something in me was softening, and when I looked at Kenzie curled up on my passenger seat, everything in me screamed to protect her.

Slowing the truck to a roll, I eased into my parking spot when we reached the cabin. I'd barely stopped before I jumped out and hurried around the truck. I didn't think it was possible, but Kenzie looked even paler than when we'd left Joe's a few minutes ago.

She moaned when I lifted her out of the truck and walked to the door. It was only when the moans became more urgent that I realized she was going to be sick. Unfortunately, by then it was too late.

Before we'd even made it into the house, Kenzie's stomach had rid itself of its contents. I looked at her shirt and then at mine and let out a groan. That she threw up on me didn't bother me half as much as needing to clean her up did.

Removing her clothes was the last thing on my mind—okay, that's a lie, but when I'd imagined it, it was under very different circumstances. I pushed through the door and with Kenzie still in my arms; headed straight to my bathroom.

I dropped the toilet seat and lowered Kenzie onto it. "Can you sit, sweetheart?" She mumbled incoherently but attempted to stay seated. Tapping her cheek gently, I waited until she opened her eyes. They were so glazed over; I doubted she'd even hear me. "I'll be right back, okay?"

As I moved to my bedroom, I pulled my shirt over my head and dropped it on the floor. I grabbed the first clean tee I could find and rushed back to the bathroom. Kenzie was still sitting on the closed toilet seat, her head resting on the tank.

While I waited for the water to get warm, memories of another time Kenzie and I were in this exact same situation tried to break free. I purposefully pushed them back; I didn't want to remember. I lathered up the cloth and then froze.

I had to undress her.

Panic danced its way down my spine. I didn't think of myself as a pervert, but I also knew how this woman affected me when she was still fully clothed. I drew strength from somewhere and focused on the task at hand.

With the hem of her shirt gripped between my fingers, I lifted the fabric up and over her head and immediately swallowed hard. I shifted her so the tank could support her back. My fingers trembled as I swiped the cloth over her chest.

I dropped to my haunches and slipped the brown leather from her feet then I proceeded to drag her jeans down her body. Now, as much as I would have liked to say that I didn't even peek at the half-naked woman sitting in my bathroom, I couldn't.

All of that creamy skin on display had me wishing she was sober just so I could taste her lips and love on her body until she was drunk from ecstasy. I let out an audible groan at the direction my thoughts were taking. I felt so conflicted. Just a few hours ago I was so mad at this woman that my vision had turned red, and now all I could think about was having her.

Maybe Kenzie wasn't the only intoxicated one?

When she was as clean as I was going to get her, I pulled my shirt over her head and gathered her up in my arms. It was only when I placed her on my bed that I noticed the butterfly tattoo on her outer thigh. She must've had it done after we broke up. I sank onto the mattress beside her to closer inspect the art.

My breath left my body in a big whoosh.

A blue butterfly with wings sprawled sat proudly on her skin. But it was the pointed edges of the wings that caused my breath to hitch. Each pointed edge curled and swirled out; one forming a *K* and the other a *B*.

When Kenzie and I had still been together, I'd drawn that butterfly for her. It was *my* design sitting on her skin, permanently branding her.

I brought my hand up and brushed my fingers over the K sitting on my chest, my heart hiccupped. As desperately as I needed air, my lungs refused to work. How the hell was it possible that after all these years, I still ached so badly?

The ink on her skin was so delicate and so beautiful—just like her—I simply had to touch. My fingers glided over the design, and when the memories begged to be set free, I closed my eyes and gave in.

"Brett, I think I'm drunk."

Kenzie swayed and tightened her hold on my arm. I pulled free and just as she began to protest, I scooped her up. "Yeah, Sweetheart, you are." She'd been doing shots with her friend, Zoe, all night and I knew they'd catch up with her at some point.

A little giggle bubbled up as she wrapped her arms around my neck. Man, it felt amazing. I hugged her closer to my chest as I took the stairs to my one-bedroom apartment two at a time. I'm not going to lie; I was nervous as hell walking through my front door.

Kenzie and I had been dating for just over six months, and she had yet to spend the night at my place, or vice versa. Although, her daddy would probably shoot me dead if I ever spent the night with her under his roof. That man did not care for me at all.

Unfortunately for him, his daughter was my world. She was so different from the other girls I'd dated; I wanted to take things slow with her.

I kicked the door shut, and Kenzie snuggled deeper into my neck for a second before her head whipped up, and she announced, "I want a puppy."

Her eyes drew me in, and all I could think was how anyone could refuse this woman anything? According to her, her parents had never allowed her to have pets of any kind while she was growing up, and seeing as she still lived under their roof, she still couldn't. But, boy did her heart ache for a puppy.

My hold on her tightened, and I silently vowed that one day, in the near future, I'd get her a puppy.

"Why are we spinning?" she whined. I bit the inside of my cheek to stop my grin from spreading. My girlfriend was stupid drunk, and all I could think was how damn cute she looked with her brows pulled together and that stubborn pout on her lips.

I placed her on the couch and moved to the kitchen to get her some water. When I came back, she was sitting with her legs tucked beneath her and looking at me funny. Handing her the water, I parked my ass on the coffee table.

Kenzie gulped down the water at an alarming pace. "Slow down, Sweetheart," I warned. "You're gonna make yourself sick." Her blue eyes sparkled with mirth as she plonked the glass down and reached forward to run her fingers up my thigh.

This time, I didn't hide my smile as she bit into her lip and batted her lashes. Turned out alcohol set the seductress in Kenzie free. Unfortunately for us both, I wasn't about to go down that route. As I said, things with her were different; I didn't want the first time we made love to be in a haze of drunkenness.

Call me whatever you want, but I loved this girl, and I was determined to do right by her. She leaned in but instead of kissing me, she threw up. Her hand flew to her mouth as she jumped up and sprinted for the bathroom

Not even caring that I was covered in sick, I stripped out of my dirty shirt and dropped it in the laundry basket as I entered the bathroom where Kenzie was heaving into the toilet. Running my hand up and down her back, I gathered as much of her hair as I could in the other.

This wasn't the most romantic setting, in fact, it was as far from romantic as you could get. But for me, this was what my future looked like: Me taking care of my girl.

When her stomach was done dispelling its contents, I pushed to my feet and turned on the faucet in the shower. As soon as the water was warm enough, I pulled Kenzie in with me—clothes and all.

Her eyes were big and filled with so many emotions. With both of my hands, I pushed her wet strands out of her face before pressing my lips to her forehead. I then took part in a true test of willpower when I began to remove the fabric that clung to her body like a second skin. Piece by piece my resolve was tested.

Now, right up until the day she died, my momma raised a gentleman. But this gentleman was still a red-blooded man, and when Kenzie stood before me wearing nothing but the skin she was born in, I couldn't not look.

She was glorious and perfect; I couldn't wait to explore every inch of creamy skin. My fingers already tingled in anticipation of feeling her silkiness beneath them and my mouth longed to commit her taste to memory.

All of that would have to wait though.

I turned off the shower, stepped out and grabbed a towel from the rack. After I wrapped Kenzie up in it, I carried her to the bedroom where I pulled one of my shirts over her head. I replaced my own wet clothes with a pair of boxer shorts before I climbed onto the bed with Kenzie.

First, I propped myself up against the headboard then I gathered her into my arms, her head resting on my chest. I drifted off to sleep feeling on top of the world.

I rubbed my chest willing the ache inside to go away. I'd much rather endure a slap to the balls than this gnawing pain that just wouldn't let up. What I needed was breathing space and no walls caging me in. I moved to get off the bed, but Kenzie murmuring my name stopped me short.

Glancing over my shoulder, I found her eyes focused on me. The tears that threatened to roll down her cheeks, giving her blue irises so much more depth. I swallowed down the urge to lunge forward and kiss both our pain away.

"Brett," she repeated, and for some reason, I held my breath. "I'm sorry I made you hate me."

Brett

"HI."

I SLOWLY PARTED MY LIDS TO FIND KENZIE'S BEAUTIFUL FACE A FEW INCHES FROM MINE. My lips stretched into an easy smile, "Hi." My heart expanded as unadulterated happiness lit up her features. I tried to push myself further up the bed, and when I had difficulty moving, I realized Kenzie was straddling me.

The slightest blush stole her cheeks while she pulled her fingers through her hair. "I used your toothbrush."

My palms ran up her arms and down again. "Sweetheart, I don't mind. What's mine is yours." The sound of her laughter brought with it peace equivalent to listening to the birds' morning song. Wrapping my arms around her, I pulled her to my chest and maneuvered into a seated position. "What's so funny, mmm?" I asked against her neck.

Her breath hitched, and I did nothing to hide my smile. She let out a little squeal when my teeth gently grazed her skin. "That's something married people say." Her words stopped me abruptly, not because they scared me. I pulled back so I could look into her eyes; search for something to tell me it was wrong to feel this strong about her, about us.

I found nothing.

Instead of telling her how I wanted nothing more than to wake up next to her every day for the rest of my life; I pressed my lips against hers. I kissed her with everything I had in me, running my tongue over her lip. Begging to not only be let into her mouth but her heart too.

While our tongues coiled together, my hands skimmed up her thighs and pushed beneath the cotton shirt. Her hips flexed, and I had to stifle a groan. My fingers dug into her soft flesh, and she rolled her hips again with more urgency this time. There was barely any fabric between us and when she pushed into me again, my fingers dug deeper, and that groan finally broke free.

Our kiss deepened, but something felt off. I sensed her hesitancy before she pulled away from me. We'd fooled around plenty of times before, but I'd never seen that worried look on her face. Afraid that I'd done something wrong, I took her face between my palms, "I'm sorry, I got carried away. It's—"

"Not you," she interrupted. "I have to tell you something." The look on her face had ice spreading in my veins.

"You can tell me anything."

She pulled her lip between her teeth and when she released it, she whispered, "Promise not to laugh."

I was still holding her face in my hands; I pulled her close, so we were nose to nose. "Sweetheart, I'll only ever laugh with *you*. Never at *you*."

Her head bobbed up and down as much as it could. I wanted to give her space, but I still needed to touch her, I dropped my hands to her outer thighs. "I've never been with anyone, Brett." She covered her face with her hands, and I barely made out her, "Gosh, this is embarrassing."

I had to admit that was unexpected. Reaching for her, I pried her hands away. I wanted to look into her eyes when I spoke. "That's something to be proud of, not ashamed." I held her gaze, making sure my words sank in. "And I will never pressure you into something you're not ready to do. What we have is enough for me."

Something flashed in her eyes, "What if I'm ready now?" Words failed me. I stared at her with my mouth hanging open like a moron. Kenzie leaned forward and pressed her lips to my cheek; my eyes closed of their own accord as I breathed her in. She moved her lips to my other cheek before brushing them over mine. "Make love to me, Brett."

Now, what sane man could resist a request like that? I searched her face for hesitancy but couldn't find a single ounce.

Her hair felt like silk as I threaded my fingers in her strands. I pulled her to me and covered her mouth with my own. The feel of her tongue lapping against mine sent shock-waves through me.

My hands slid down her back until it reached the hem of her shirt, I waited a second before I pulled it over her head and threw it to the floor. I flipped us over, pushed onto my knees so I could properly admire the beauty before me.

Her thick mass of chocolate hair fell like a halo around her head, and it was fitting. By all accounts, she was an angel, my saving grace. I'd found her when I thought I'd lost everything. My gaze set off at a slow perusal of her magnificent body. I didn't know what I did to deserve her, but there was no way I was ever letting her go.

I kissed every inch of skin on display, and it didn't matter how desperately I needed it, I didn't take my own pleasure until she was satisfied two times over. When I finally covered her body with mine, I knew that I would never be the same again. She gave me the most precious gift, and in return, I gave her my heart.

Breathless, we toppled over. Our limbs, much like our souls, a tangled mess. I pushed onto my elbow and immediately got lost in Kenzie's eyes. "You okay?" I asked after a few breaths.

She beamed up at me, causing my heart to swell. After she lifted onto her elbow too, she pressed her mouth to mine for a quick kiss. Her breath blew over my lips as she whispered, "Perfect."

Gently, I brushed her hair away from her face and tucked it behind her ear. "You're so damn beautiful," I murmured against her lips. Resisting the urge to kiss her senseless, I pulled back slightly to watch the blush settle in her cheeks, and her lips lift into a shy smile.

"I love it when you look at me like that," she confessed.

"Like what?"

Kenzie's smile grew even wider. "Like I'm your entire world, and you can't bear to let me go."

I brushed my fingertips over her cheek, "You are and I can't." Pushing my fingers into her hair, I cupped the back of her head and pulled her face to mine. Against her mouth, I pleaded, "Tell me you'll always be mine?"

"Forever," feather-soft kisses stole my breath, "I'll love you forever, Brett."

I woke with a start, my heart desperately trying to get out of my chest. My eyes snapped to the bed, and a sigh of relief escaped when I saw that Kenzie was asleep. Her words still echoed in my mind. I wanted to tell her that I could never hate her. As I watched her sleeping form, my fingers twitched, they ached to touch her, to feel her.

The walls around me shifted, and I couldn't breathe. I jumped up and didn't stop running until everything burned. Twigs and leaves crunched beneath my feet, my chest heaved, and breathing became near impossible. Still, I didn't stop.

Eventually, my legs gave out, and I dropped to my knees. With my head hanging, I begged for the ache in me to go away. It was as if all the pain and anger I'd stored away for years came rushing out of me in one fell swoop and it was too much to handle.

Tiny bursts of sunlight came filtering through the trees and with it brought some clarity. I could run as fast and as far as my feet would carry me, but I could never outrun my love for Kenzie.

KENZIE

WHY WAS MY BRAIN TRYING TO BREAK OUT OF MY SKULL? I covered my head with my hands and slowly pried my lids apart only to snap them shut again. Bright yellow rays mercilessly blinded me. My tongue and cheeks were replaced with cotton balls, and a desert had taken up residence in my throat.

What the hell happened?

I tried to remember, but my mind kept drawing up a blank; the splitting ache above my brows not helping matters at all.

Focus, dammit.

Nothing but a big black hole sat where my memory should've been. Panic forced my lids apart, and despite the stinging in my eyes and throbbing of my skull, I sat up. As my blurred surroundings became clear, my heart thundered in my chest.

I gathered the gray sheet in my hands and clutched it close to my body as I scanned the unfamiliar room. A wooden desk stood in front of a large window covered with blinds that were only half open. I squinted to try to make out what was beyond the glass but other than a few trees, I saw nothing.

I turned my attention to the opposite side of the room and there, too, was a blind-covered window. In front of it stood a ball foot dresser in rich mahogany and an oval-shaped single-seater. Terrified, I dropped the sheet and almost screamed when I noticed I wasn't wearing my clothes but rather something that looked like a man's t-shirt.

What did I do?

Shame bubbled to the surface and stung the back of my eyes. I'd always prided myself in the fact that I wasn't a one-night stand girl or a cheating one. Apparently, I'd been wrong. Angrily, I swiped at the tears trickling down my cheeks.

No use in crying now. I had to pull up my big-girl panties and face the consequences of my actions—whoever he may've been. Gingerly, I slipped from the bed and scanned the floor for strewn about clothes and found nothing.

I rushed to the door, pulled it open and slammed straight into a six-foot-three wall of wet muscle.

Wait, what?

The first thing that came into view was my spread fingers on top of some very fine pecs. My gaze traveled up, and I bit the inside of my cheek to stop myself from gasping at the sight of Brett staring down at me, brows drawn together and jaw ticking.

I tried to step back, and when I couldn't, I realized his arm snaking around my waist tethered me to him. The muscles in his chest jumped, it took all my willpower not to flex my fingers and test them.

We were standing so close that I could see his nostrils flare and I bet he could hear my heart's wild gallop. My mouth suddenly felt even drier than it had when I'd woken up a couple of minutes ago. I slid my tongue over my lips, and immediately Brett's eyes followed the action. I saw him work down a swallow before his ticking jaw picked up speed.

Brett released me and took a few steps back, but his gaze lingered, slowly traveling the length of me. He dragged a hand through his damp hair before he shoved both into his sweatpants' pockets. My eyes were drawn to the 'K' inked on his chest and then the beads of sweat sliding down his skin, disappearing into his pants.

I swallowed hard.

"How are you feeling?" His voice sounded strained.

Wrapping my arms around myself, I confessed, "Besides the fact that elephants are doing the can-can inside my skull, I don't remember a thing."

Eyes narrowed, he studied me for a few seconds. "Nothing?"

The way he asked it made my skin tingle with uneasiness. Again, I was left with the same question, "What happened last night? The last thing I remember was telling Lizzy and Harper I felt sick."

Brett seemed lost in thought as he glanced out the window. Looking back at me, he shrugged his shoulders. "Those cocktails are pretty strong and as I recall, you never really could handle your drink."

I wanted to stand tall and protest, but he wasn't wrong. In fact, the only other time I'd been drunk was when I was with him. Memories of the morning after came rushing back, and I had to avert my gaze.

Everything from that morning was so ingrained in me, I swear if I closed my eyes I'd still be able to feel his hands gliding along my skin and his mouth teasing me, tasting me. That morning wasn't only the first time we'd made love, but it was also when I'd learned that sex was about so much more than two people seeking a release. It was about hearts intertwining and souls weaving together.

"Take these."

I blinked, and Brett stood before me, two tiny pills in one hand and bottled water in the other. Apparently, I'd been so lost in my thoughts that I hadn't even heard him move. "How did I end up here—" I looked down at the shirt I was wearing, "—wearing this?"

Brett's eyes flitted to the pills in his hand before his gaze met mine again. Only when I took the medication did he speak, "Mrs. D doesn't like it when her guests show up drunk," he shrugged again as if his rising and falling shoulders were all the explanation I needed. "As for the shirt, I couldn't let you sleep covered in sick."

By my apparent behavior, one would think I was back in College. I immediately thought of my parents and Dean and how ashamed they'd be of me. Purposefully, I searched Brett's eyes for something that resembled shame or even anger, but to my surprise, I didn't find it.

What I did find was perplexing, to say the least.

I shook my head, thinking my very hungover mind was playing tricks on me. There was no way that I'd seen longing in his eyes. I checked again, just to be sure but this time I was met with an emotionless veil.

Brett stepped back and headed toward his kitchen, I followed. He opened the fridge and soon disappeared from view. Feeling a little less intimidated, I muttered, "Thank you." A second later he reappeared, his arms loaded with food only barely hiding that delectable chest of his.

"No thanks needed," he said dryly as he placed eggs, tomatoes, and capsicums on the counter. "I just did what any decent person would." He moved to the other side of the kitchen where he grabbed two onions and a few spice bottles. Those, too, joined the rest of the items on the counter.

That awkwardness was back again, and as I looked around his cozy little kitchen, I found myself jealous of the woman who got to share this space with him. A frown formed on my forehead, I shouldn't be thinking or feeling things like that. "Lola isn't mad?"

He gave me a look that said it really wasn't any of my business and because I knew he was right, I nodded my head. "I should probably go. If I could get my clothes…?"

The knife in his hand stilled. "You're not leaving until you've eaten something. Your clothes are still in the dryer, but you're welcome to take a shower while you wait."

I was probably stuck in some weird dream from which I couldn't wake up. In my reality, there was no way Brett Carter would've carted me home and taken care of me. Glancing down at the shirt, I realized he most likely had to change me. Everything he was doing verged on being sweet, and I knew for a fact that this man didn't care for me.

That left only one question.

"I thought you hated me. Why are you being so nice all of a sudden?"

A pained expression pulled his brows together and drew his eyes closed. Brett let out a slow breath before he opened his eyes again. "I don't hate you, Kenzie." The softness of his voice wrapped itself around me like a blanket in the winter. "I was—*I am*—angry. I went to jail *for you*. I never expected you to wait for me, but I at least thought that when the time came, you'd tell me to my face that you were moving on." He dropped the knife and raked his hand through his hair while he turned his back to me. "Look, let's leave the past where it belongs. You're here, for what, another night at most? I think we can be civil with each other until you leave, don't you?"

I was so confused by his statement. What did he mean? He was the one who broke up with me. I'd written him a letter a day, explaining that my parents had forbidden me to go see him. The one time I tried, I hadn't even made it past the front gate—my dad's connections stretched far. After seven months of not hearing a damn thing, a letter showed up out of the blue. I was so excited when I recognized Brett's handwriting on the envelope, but when I'd opened it, my whole life came crashing down around me.

...I could never live with you in my life ever again...

I swallowed down the lump in my throat that always came when I thought of that letter. I was good with not talking about the past.

"A shower sounds great."

Chapter 14

BRETT

I WAS ROOTED TO THE SPOT AS I WATCHED KENZIE SPIN ON HER HEELS and march down the short hallway. This whole situation confused the heck out of me. Why did she look so perplexed a few moments ago? I wasn't proud of the last things I'd said—or rather wrote—to her. If I could, I'd take them all back, but I thought that she'd at least have a little comprehension for where it came from.

By the looks of it, she didn't.

Shaking my head, I picked up the knife and continued chopping up the breakfast ingredients. Over the past years I'd nursed more than my fair share of hangovers and what Kenzie needed was a decent meal to replace all those lost nutrients.

The sound of water running caught my attention, and I did my best not to envision tiny droplets of water sliding down her skin or the way she looked lathering up her body. I swallowed down the string of curses that were on the tip of my tongue.

What was it with this woman that suddenly kicked my libido into high gear? I'd already had trouble focusing this morning when all of her softness was pressed up against me. And don't even get me started on how gorgeous she looked wearing nothing but a confused look and my t-shirt.

Somewhere between yesterday morning and me taking care of Kenzie, something had shifted, and my emotions were all over the damn place. One moment I wanted to yell at her for all the hurt she'd caused; in the next, I wanted to kiss her, long and hard, until she forgot the asshole waiting for her back home.

My grip around the knife tightened as the simmering anger came to a boil…*again.* I envied her ability to move on with her life, and I was pissed beyond belief that I was still so stuck in the past that *my life* had become nothing more than moving from one moment to the next.

I could deny it from here till Sunday, but the truth was, I wanted what Logan and Harper had. I'd always wanted that. As I scraped the chopped vegetables into a bowl, I recalled how easy it had been to plan a future with Kenzie in it. The moment I'd laid eyes on her, she'd become the center of my universe.

In my mind, we could weather any storm. It didn't matter that we came from different backgrounds or that her daddy didn't want us together. We'd had each other, and that'd been enough.

Until it wasn't.

I cracked the eggs one by one into a separate bowl, and after adding a little milk, I whisked them with more force than was necessary.

"Can I help?"

Kenzie's voice stilled my actions, and even though I didn't want to, I made myself look up. She was standing in the doorway, looking a little lost and a whole lot sexy. Thick, damp strands spilled over her shoulder, staining the fabric beneath it.

My teeth dug into the inside of my cheek as my gaze swept over her. It wasn't difficult to notice that she was sans bra and when I caught sight of all the leg she had on display—courtesy of my shirt ending mid-thigh—all I could think about was having them wrapped around me.

The need to stomp over to her and plunge my tongue into her pretty little mouth was almost unbearable. I wanted to run my fingers up her bare thighs and lift her onto the nearest surface where I could ravish her until my name left her lungs in a breathy whisper.

Shifting from one foot to the other, I was thankful that I was standing behind the island; there was no hiding how she affected me.

"I think I've got it." I feigned a cough to hide the hoarseness in my voice.

"What happened to your hand?"

I looked at my knuckles and shrugged, "Nothing."

"Oh." Her eyes darted from one item to the next as she scanned my kitchen, and I couldn't help but wonder what she made of its simplicity. A counter ran along the length of one wall with cabinets above it; although the rest of the cabin was furnished with dark stained wood, I'd gone for a light one in here.

The island on which I was working also held the stove, and behind me was my favorite part of the cabin. An entire wall made of glass ensured that I'd never felt caged while in here. The endless stretch of trees, beyond the window, calmed me almost as much as running or working with glass did.

"You don't mind, do you?"

I blinked. Was she speaking this entire time? "Mind what?"

The slightest pink tinged her cheeks. Man, that brought back a whole lot of memories. I swallowed them down and willed something else to go down too.

"There was an unopened toothbrush in the bathroom cupboard," she pulled her lip between her teeth for a second before she hurried on, "I'll replace it."

I knew I was a bastard, but for some reason, I didn't want Kenzie to know the real reason why there was a boxed toothbrush under my sink. "You should drink that," Ignoring the tug inside my chest, I pointed to the poured orange juice on the counter. "If your stomach can handle food, I'll make coffee."

She gave me a quick nod and padded toward the counter. I couldn't help staring after her. There was something about having her in my space that felt… *Right?* I shook my head at the thought. Clearly, I'd gone and lost my damned mind.

"It's not that I don't appreciate what you've done, 'cause I do," My gaze locked with Kenzie's. "I just think it's best I get going. Last night things already seemed heated, and I really would hate if I caused any trouble between you and—"

Biting back a smile, I cocked my head to the side while she rambled on. Maybe it was because my mind had already left me, but her going on like that had to be the cutest thing I'd ever seen. If I'd had a little less willpower, I'd march over there and kiss the words right out of her mouth.

That thought had my eyes dropping to her moving lips; I swear I could already taste the orange juice on them. My tongue snaked over my own lips, and hers stopped moving. Slowly, I lifted my gaze to hers only to find that she was staring at *my* mouth.

Maybe she was as affected by me as I was by her? "Lola and I aren't dating," and before I could check myself, I continued, "We just…"

My voice trailed off, and as realization set in, her eyes grew wide, and her head snapped toward the bedroom. "Oh."

I planted my palms on the smooth wooden surface and sighed. There was nothing to be ashamed of; I was a grown-ass man with needs. And I had every damn right in the world to have those needs tended to.

So why the hell did I feel like a piece of shit?

She was right. She should leave. Only, I couldn't tell her that because I knew that when she walked out that door, I'd never see her again. She'd go back to her perfect life, and I would still be left behind.

KENZIE

"SO…" I LOOKED EVERYWHERE EXCEPT AT BRETT. The entire morning had been filled with nothing but awkward moments; this one the worst of them all. We'd gone from screwing each other with our eyes, to not being able to make eye-contact within a second flat.

I was still reeling from the heat in his eyes that set my pulse on fire from across the room when he'd announced that Lola wasn't his girlfriend. Obviously, that news shouldn't make me want to smile, but dammit, it did. I hated myself a little for it, too.

My reaction also confused the heck out of me. It had me questioning not only my loyalty, but my entire relationship with Dean. If he was the one I was supposed to be with, would Brett still have affected me this way? Or did Brett affect me this way because I had never truly let him go? I mean, checking up on your ex regularly was not exactly moving on.

"So…?" Brett echoed my one-word sentence.

I should say something…anything. "Nice place you have here." *Really?* That's what my brain came up with? Resisting the urge to roll my eyes at myself, I brought the juice to my lips and swallowed down the tangy sweetness, that way my mouth was too busy to spew out more word-vomit.

His sandy brows pulled together, and his lips twitched, almost as if he was holding back a smile. "Thanks," he grabbed the bowl of eggs and continued to whisk them. "It'd taken a lot of convincin' and a few of Mrs. Jackson's pecan pies, but eventually the town council agreed to sell me this patch of land to build on."

"You built this cabin?" I couldn't hide the surprise in my voice.

Pride softened his features, and his eyes turned the color of honey. "Sure did," he set the bowl back on the counter and pulled a pan from the cupboard beneath it. "Logan and his brothers helped with some of the heavy lifting."

It wasn't difficult to imagine the four of them working on the cabin, drinking beers and just being men. Again, I found myself envious of the life he'd built in Willow Creek.

A life he'd built without me in it.

I turned and pretended to inspect something on the countertop to hide the sudden sadness that had fallen over me. I was being silly. It wasn't his fault that I was holding onto the past with both my hands.

When I looked up, the big window behind him caught my attention. It wasn't so much a window as it was a wall of glass, but the view was magnificent. I moved without thinking, I only stopped when I was close enough to brush my fingers over the glass.

Trees stretched as far as I could see, slivers of light filtering through here and there. I felt a sense of freedom wash over me as I took in the breathtaking panorama. Even with all the foliage surrounding it, the cabin didn't seem dark or gloomy.

It felt like home.

"I can't stand to be in a place without windows." At the sound of Brett's voice, I turned around only to find him a few inches from me, his focus was where mine had been a moment ago. "I need space, and the houses in town don't provide nearly enough of it."

Something clicked into place, and I finally understood. I could even accept that the insults he'd thrown at me in his letter were warranted. I *had* been selfish. Not once did I consider what he went through or what he had to give up because of me.

I reached forward and flattened my palm against his bare chest. He jerked, and when his gaze snapped to mine, his eyes looked wild. "Brett, I realize I should have said this a long time ago, and that it doesn't make anything better but, I truly am sorry for everything you've lost because I wasn't woman enough to fight my own battles."

He swallowed hard, and the hurt he felt showed in his eyes. "I never finished my studies, never became the artist I'd wanted to be." His jaw muscle started to jump. "Lost my friends, had to move away and start my life from scratch." I felt the tears roll down my cheeks as his pained words lodged in my chest. "But don't you see, Kenzie," he cupped my face, his eyes searching mine. "None of that compares to losing—"

He snatched his hands from me and took a step back; his breaths coming in quick successions. "I can't do this now." He shook his head and took another step backward before he spun around and stormed off.

I pressed my palm to my stomach as I was showered with guilt. Guilt over everything Brett had to endure, and guilt for wanting him to finish his sentence and tell me that losing me had crippled him, as much as losing him had broken me.

What was I thinking? I thought that by seeing him and talking to him, I'd get closure. The only thing I got was a whole heap of confusion. I blew out a long, slow breath and took in the uncooked ingredients on the counter.

Might as well make myself useful.

First, I hunted for plates; opening up almost all the cupboards before I found them. Then I scavenged his fridge for cheese. I had no idea what breakfast he'd had in mind, but I was making omelets.

When life hands you broken eggs and all…

Just as I slid the last one onto the plate, Brett's presence filled the kitchen. I didn't have to look to know his eyes were on me, I felt it. My skin felt as though someone had pressed a live wire to it. After sucking in some much-needed air, I turned my eyes to the entryway.

That emotionless mask that he wore so well was back and he'd finally covered up all the skin he'd had on display.

I opened my mouth to speak, but he was faster. "I appreciate the apology, but I think we should leave the past where it belongs. It's been twelve years and I really just want to forget it ever happened." Brett moved farther into the kitchen and lifted his arm. Only then did I spot my clothes hanging from it. "It's dry."

Nodding, I took that as his subtle way of telling me I wasn't wanted there. My feet felt heavy as I moved to take my jeans and tank from him. "Thanks," I mumbled.

He regarded me through slightly narrowed eyes, and when I finally couldn't handle his gaze on me anymore, I rushed off. Just before I entered the room, I noticed the hole in the door and I wondered if his bruised hand had anything to do with it.

As I stepped into my jeans, I recalled that his hand wasn't hurt when I'd seen him at the guesthouse on Sunday. I pulled my tank over my head and stuffed my bra in my back pocket. Over my shoulder, I glanced at the closed door before I pulled on the bedside table drawer.

I should have known it would be filled with the kind of things single, virile men keep close to the bed; I just wasn't prepared to be bombarded with all the stuff that would make for one kinky night.

That's what I get for snooping.

With a lot more force than was called for, I slammed the offending drawer shut and immediately jumped to face the door. I didn't want to get caught rummaging through things I had no business looking at in the first place.

The only problem now was every time I looked at Brett, I would know what was in his drawer, and then my stupid imagination would probably create some very vivid images.

Ugh! The sooner I left, the better.

"So, I'll just be on my way then," I announced when I re-entered the kitchen.

Brett looked up from where he was filling two glasses with more orange juice. He turned his gaze to the ceiling and sighed heavily. "First breakfast," he insisted when his attention was on me again. "Then I will drop you off at the guesthouse."

"Oh no, I don't want to put you out any more than I already have." Being stubborn was new to me. I threw my thumb over my shoulder, "I'll find my way."

Brett's chuckle filled the room; I hated it for warming my insides like it did. "Kenzie, sit and eat your breakfast. We'll leave after."

My brows pulled together, and I planted my hands on my hips. "I'm leaving now."

His sandy strands spilled over his forehead as he shook his head with annoyance. "Fine, you wanna walk fifteen miles, be my guest." With his plate and glass in hand, he pushed past me and plonked down at the dinette. "Your phone and the cash you had on you are on the bookcase." He pointed toward said bookcase with his knife before he continued to shovel food into his mouth.

Fifteen miles? I wasn't an athlete, but I did keep fit by running and taking spinning classes three times a week. To walk fifteen miles just seemed so daunting in my current state.

My gaze bounced from Brett, to the plate of food on the counter, to the door, before it settled on the food again. Gingerly, I grabbed the omelet and juice and joined Brett at the table.

"Not a word," I grumbled around a bite of food.

We ate in silence, stealing glances at each other every few minutes. I had no idea what else to say. The least I could do was respect his wish and not bring up the past, I owed him that much. The only problem was, that was all that was on my mind. I wanted to know why the only time he ever wrote to me was to tell me how much better his life would have been if he'd never met me.

When his plate was empty, Brett stood. I felt his gaze and had no other choice than to return it. "I'm sweaty and dirty."

I blinked and willed my eyes to stay glued to his. "W-what now?"

"You know, from my run earlier." When all I could do was nod, he continued. "Would you mind if I took a quick shower before we left?"

Can I help? I bit my tongue before the words slipped out and shook my head. I wished my brain would stop going into schoolgirl-mode around him. Brett tilted his head to the side and frowned. It looked as if he was trying to piece together an intricate puzzle.

"Well, okay then." He turned and headed down the hall but stopped midway. Glancing over his shoulder, he reminded me, "Don't forget your stuff on the bookcase."

The bathroom door clicked, and I let out a breath I had no idea I was holding. I cursed my silly hormones all the way to the kitchen where I rinsed the dirty dishes and tried my hardest not to think about a very naked Brett in the shower.

He is taking an awfully long time in there…

Ugh! I needed a distraction. That was when I remembered my phone. Crossing the room, I snatched my stuff from the shelf, pocketed the few notes and powered up my phone. No sooner had the light come on, when the thing started to buzz uncontrollably due to all the messages filtering in.

A total of ten missed calls were noted along with eight text messages. Apparently, Dean, my parents, and Zoe had been looking for me. That was a whole other mess I needed to clean up. Deciding I'd deal with them once I was back at the guesthouse, I slid my phone into my pocket and paused.

How did I not see them earlier?

Butterflies, they were everywhere. Different colors, different sizes. A small blue one closest to the edge caught my attention, and I couldn't help myself, I picked it up. It was beautiful, and it made my heart ache. The delicate piece of glass resting in my palm held my attention hostage. A million things racing through my mind, and a myriad of emotions flooding through me.

"You made this," I stated when the sound of Brett's footfalls reached my ears. For the first time in what felt like minutes, I looked up and scanned the butterflies before me. "You made them all."

He moved with the grace of a cat as he approached me; with every step he took, my heart beat faster. Brett took the tiny sculpture from my hand and returned it to its spot. He didn't look at me, and I wasn't sure if it was because he couldn't or wouldn't.

"These are amazing, Brett." I moved closer to him and placed my hand on his arm. The muscles beneath my fingers twitched. "You shouldn't be working in an auto shop when you have so much talent just…" my voice trailed off as I tried to find the right words to say.

He pulled away from my touch, and I frowned. "So much talent just what, Kenzie?" His voice had an edge to it; clearly I'd hit a nerve without intending to. "Wasting away? Yeah, you *would* think that."

"What the hell is wrong with you?" I turned away from him and shook my head. "You're so thickheaded, you know that? I was trying to compliment you."

"*You* are what's wrong with me!" His voice reverberated off the walls. "You're so damn infuriating. One moment I want to grab you by the shoulders and shake some sense into you and the next, I want to—"

He stopped abruptly, and I spun back around. The veins in his neck bulged and his jaw muscle bounced again. "You want to what?" A verbal confirmation wasn't necessary; the heat in his eyes told me all I needed to know. Still, I wanted it.

Better yet, I wanted him to act on it.

He didn't though. "Nothing," he mumbled as he turned and stomped toward the door. "You ready to leave?"

Boy, was I ever.

BRETT

THE LOUD SLAM OF MY TRUCK DOOR SIGNALED KENZIE'S EXIT. Instead of spinning away like I wanted to, I sat behind the wheel until she disappeared behind the front door of the guesthouse. My gaze traveled to the top windows of the two-story building, and I wondered which one of the rooms was Kenzie's.

With a shake of my head, I threw the truck into gear and eased away from the curb. A smile stretched across my lips as I replayed most of the morning's events. One thing was certain; Kenzie had become feisty over the years. I could still see her hands planted on her hips and determination flashing in her eyes.

My smile faltered when I recalled how the tears rolled down her cheeks. Things had been intense, for sure. The way she'd looked at me just before we left the cabin had my insides twisting and I'd almost—*almost*—given in and kissed the fight out of her.

I pulled up in front of the shop and scolded myself; I needed to stop thinking about having my mouth on her or how glorious it would be to sink— "You're late." Logan mocked from the sidewalk.

Purposefully, I slowly unfolded myself from the cab. "Oh wait, I have something for you," I made a show of searching through my pockets before I withdrew my hand, middle finger in the air.

Logan snorted, "Ha ha, funny."

I smiled my first genuine smile in a couple of days and took the coffee my friend held out.

"How's Kenzie doing?"

"She's probably feeling those cocktails right about now."

Logan grinned; we'd both had our fair share of hangovers. "Did you tell her that Lola spiked her drinks?"

"Nah," I shook my head and opened the lid of the coffee cup. After giving it a blow, I explained, "No need to rock a boat that don't need rockin'."

"I hear ya, man." Mrs. Henderson came crawling down the road in her husband's old Chev, both Logan and I waved as she passed us by. "What are you going to do about it?"

Brows drawn, I side-eyed my friend. "About what?"

"This thing with Lola? Clearly, there's some stuff you need to sort out."

Dragging my hand through my hair, I sighed. "Dunno." A yawn broke free, and I covered my mouth with my hand. I would've preferred my tiredness came from something other than sex dreams about my ex.

"Long night?" he asked.

"Long morning." I fell into step next to Logan and brought the to-go cup to my lips before I took a long swallow. I needed something stronger than caffeine to help me regain my focus—or rather help me forget.

"So it's like that now?" He teased when we entered the shop.

I came to an abrupt halt and glared at him. "No, it's definitely not like *that*." I ground my teeth together. "That woman is just so…so…"

"Infuriating?"

"Yes!"

"Drives you up the walls?"

"Abso-friggin-lutely."

"And all you can think about is kissing her until she sees reason?"

"Yes…wait… No."

Logan's laughter filled the air, and by the look on his face, one would think he'd just won a prize. "What's so damn funny?"

In the distance, I heard the delivery van pulling up in front of the shop. My idiot friend smacked me on the shoulder as he walked by. I stomped over to the backroom, and while I exchanged my Levi's and tee for coveralls, I couldn't help but think about the past.

I had this gnawing feeling inside of me that there was more to it than Kenzie just casting me aside. I didn't know, maybe it was just wishful thinking due to the floodgate of emotions that had suddenly been opened. The only thing I did know for sure was that I wanted the air cleared between her and me before she left.

"Well, this is a first." Logan leaned against the doorframe.

"What?"

"Ned actually understood the term 'rush-order' for a change. The Mazda's parts just arrived."

Disappointment rushed through my veins like wildfire. "Great." I pushed past him and made my way to Kenzie's car. The job wasn't that huge which meant she'd probably be on her way out of town by nightfall.

"This doesn't mean she has to leave, you can always—"

"When did I grow a damn tail?" I interrupted Logan, irritation evident in my voice.

He held his hands up, palms facing me. "I'm just sayin', man."

"Yeah well, go say what it is you want to say to someone else."

Without another word, he stalked off and left me to work on the car, and stew. I was about halfway done with the job when lunchtime rolled around. I'd fully intended to work through lunch, but when Logan suggested that we head to the diner instead, I agreed.

The fact that Kenzie might be there had nothing to do with my decision.

"Brett?"

I looked up from where I was washing my hands. Lola stood a few feet away. In all the time I'd known her, I'd never seen her looking so unsure of herself. Her hands were clasped before her and her gaze bounced from one place to the next.

"You ready?" Already dressed, Logan stepped out of the backroom.

I shook my head, "Go ahead, I'll catch up."

He opened his mouth but didn't say anything; instead, he headed out after giving both Lola and me a curt nod.

She took a step forward, "I wanted to apologize."

"It's not me you should be apologizing to." I crossed my arms in front of me. "What was up with that, anyway?"

She pulled her shoulders up and dropped them quickly. "You've been acting weird ever since she came to town and I saw the way you were looking at her. I guess I was jealous."

I squeezed my eyes shut and pinched the bridge of my nose. "I never misled you, Lola," I mumbled on a sigh. "I have always been upfront about what I can give you." I shoved my hands into my pockets, my gaze drifted to Kenzie's car.

"I know." There was a moment of silence before she went on. "I saw you drop her off this morning."

My eyes snapped to Lola's, "And?"

"I was just wondering if she's the reason you won't let anyone in?"

My head fell back, and I stared at the wooden beams that formed part of the trusses. "You already know the answer to that." I dragged my hand through my hair and checked the time on the wall mounted clock. I was at a loss as to what to say. *'I'm sorry I couldn't reciprocate your feelings'* just didn't seem right.

"There is someone out there that is just waiting to find you, Lo." I finally said. "It's just not me."

"I hope you're right."

With heavy shoulders, she turned and left. I felt like the world's biggest douche bag; I probably was.

By the time I entered the diner, I was beyond depleted. I wanted to go back to a time where I could just switch my emotions off, but unfortunately for me, it wasn't that easy anymore. Everyone, except Eli, was huddled together in a booth, and by the way they immediately stopped talking when they spotted me, I knew I was the topic of the day.

"Y'all have nothing better to do than gossip all day?" My quip earned me an eye roll from Lizzy and a shake of Harper's head. I slid into the booth and knew they saw right through my fake smile. I snatched the coke in front of Lizzy and gulped it down.

"Hey! That's mine."

I flashed her a smile. "What are ya gonna do about it?"

"The better question is," Logan piped up. "What are you going to do about your little situation?"

"Ooh, are we talking about the Kenzie situation or the Lola one?" Harper asked.

Again, Logan was on the receiving end of my glare, but all he did was shrug his shoulders. "What? There are no secrets between Harper and me." He pulled her close and kissed the top of her head. "Right, Sugar?"

She formed a circle with her fingers and nodded. "Zero."

"Well, Lizzy and I aren't sleeping with Logan," this came from Chase. "Wanna fill us in?"

Logan and I spoke at the same time.

"Yes."

"No."

The man that was supposed to be my best friend laughed and then turned to his brother and asked, "You know that *K* he has inked on his chest?" Chase nodded, and Logan lifted one eyebrow, "Well…"

Lizzy's eyes grew wide as she bounced on the spot. "Oooooh."

"I still don't get it," Chase groaned.

A French fry flew across the table courtesy of Harper. "It stands for Kenzie, you dummy."

"Ah, so she's the one who…" Chase's voice trailed off as he glanced at me. I'd never been one to sit around and talk about my personal life, but apparently, one night when I'd had a little too much to drink, I'd told the guys that a girl broke my heart. Luckily, I never went into details, but that didn't stop them from mocking me.

They'd given me shit over it for weeks.

"Well if you ask me," Harper chimed in. "Fate had a hand in her ending up in Willow Creek."

"You believe in that mumbo jumbo?" I asked.

Her lips lifted into a smile as she looked up at Logan. "I do." My friend tugged her even closer, and despite the protests around the table, he kissed her as if none of us were watching.

I couldn't look away. The ache in my chest grew to the point of becoming unbearable the longer I stared. It was finally time, to be honest, with myself at least. I might've been furious with Kenzie, and I definitely said some shit just to hurt her right back, but there wasn't a day that went by that I didn't think about her. No matter how hard I'd tried, my love for her wouldn't diminish.

And now that I'd seen her, held her, there was not a damn thing I wouldn't do to have her look at me the way Harper looked at Logan.

What if Harper was right, and I was handed a second chance?

KENZIE

"UGH."

I fell onto the bed, face first. The entire drive back to the guesthouse, all I wanted to do was crawl into Brett's lap and just forget reality. I'd wanted to pull on the handbrake and demand he reacted on the heat I'd seen in his eyes.

Now, with my face buried in a pillow, all I wanted to do was scream until my lungs gave out. My phone *bzz bzz'd* in my pocket, interrupting my pity-party. With a very unladylike groan, I rolled onto my back and pulled the device from my jeans.

My parents' home number flashed on my screen, and I knew it was time to be an adult and face the music. I closed my eyes and answered.

"Kenzie, why have you not been answering our calls? Your father and I have been worried sick."

"You're sure daddy isn't just worried about me losing this account for the company?"

My mom gasped. "You know you are more important to him than his clients."

Pushing off the bed, I headed to the window that overlooked the garden. With my shoulder propped against the wall, I pulled the curtain back and stared at Mrs. Davis's gazebo. "I'm fine, Mom."

"Well, you don't sound it." After a few seconds of silence, my mother sighed and continued in a hushed tone, "You know the Raymonds from across the street?" She didn't give me any time to confirm. "I heard their oldest daughter suffered a breakdown after she turned thirty. Is this what's happening to you?"

My mother was well-known for her dramatics. I shook my head and then realized she couldn't see me. "My car suffered a breakdown, not me. Besides, I'm thirty-three, Mom. I think if I were going to have a meltdown over turning thirty, it would've happened by now."

"Where is this attitude coming from?"

I blew out a long breath, "I'm not giving—"

"Dean said you were at a bar. A bar, Kenzie?" *Here we go.* "Care to explain yourself?"

As usual, my statement over my age went over my mother's head. The only thing she really cared about was me making them look bad. *We have a reputation to uphold after all*. Those words were ingrained in me for as long as I could remember. When I was just a little girl, and my friends were climbing trees and playing in the mud, I had to sit stock-still next to my mother while she drank tea with her so-called-friends. *That is not lady-like behavior, Kenzie* was her response every time I'd asked if I could go play too.

I smiled as I remembered the day I'd introduced Brett to my parents. My poor mother took one look at his ratty jeans and wild hair and shook her perfectly styled head.

"You need to leave that town," I heard her say. "When are you coming home?"

"I'm not sure." I caught sight of Mrs. Davis tending to the flowers by the gazebo, and I remembered the look on her face when she spoke about her late husband. "I'm going down to the shop in a bit to find out how long my car is going to take. I'll call you later."

"Good. And for the love of all things that are holy, call Dean. That poor man is worried sick about you."

More like my parents were worried about what it would mean for my dad's company if Dean and I broke up. The firm where he worked used Renowned Eminence whenever one of the senior partners screwed up—which was very often.

"I will."

After I hung up, I watched Mrs. Davis some more. She seemed so peaceful; I wanted to borrow some of it. My phone was still clutched in my hand; I scrolled to my gallery and flicked through the photos on it.

How sad was it that the only spontaneous snaps I had were of Zoe and me? I paused at a picture of Dean and me at a work function. The smile on my face seemed forced, and my body was stiff; I looked uncomfortable.

The truth descended on me so fast; a gasp tore from my throat, and the device in my hand tumbled to the ground. Shame washed over me as I finally realized that I wasn't in love with him anymore, that I hadn't been for a long time. But because it made my parents happy, I'd stayed with him.

No more.

Things in my life needed to change. I'd just told my mother that I was a thirty-three-year-old woman. It was time I started acting like one.

I hated how the bell above the diner door drew everyone's attention to me. As I walked toward the counter, I searched for Lizzy, but a dark-haired woman was busy serving customers.

Slipping onto the stool, I was greeted with "I'll be right with ya." While I waited, I pulled out my phone and sent a text to Zoe, filling her in on everything that'd happened. After the call from my mom, I didn't have the strength for any more conversations.

"Hey, Kenzie."

I turned my phone's screen off and looked up to find Chase leaning against the counter next to me. "Hi."

"So, a few of us are here for lunch," he looked over his shoulder in the direction I assumed the lunch party was. When he turned his attention back to me he seemed a bit over excited, "C'mon, you're sitting with us."

"Do I have a say in the matter?"

He shook his head adamantly, "Nope." Turning his attention to the woman behind the counter, "Hey Dawn, she's moving to our table."

Much like last night, I followed Chase as he led me to their booth. We rounded the corner, and I immediately locked eyes with Brett. The closer we got to the table the more desperately my heart tried to break out of my chest.

"Look who I ran into." Again, Chase seemed rather overly cheery. I looked around the table at Logan, Harper and Lizzy, and they were all sporting knowing smiles. An uneasy feeling sprouted at the base of my skull and wiggled its way down my spine.

"Brett, move your ass that-a-way so the lady can sit," Chase ordered.

I was about to protest when genuine surprise stole the words from my mouth. Without so much as a grunt, Brett slid out of the booth. Confusion had me rooted to the spot. It was only when he leaned forward and whispered, "I have to sit at the end," that I regained my mobility.

The booth wasn't exactly small, but when you had three six-foot-something men squeezed in there too, it was bound to be a tight fit. So tight that even though my legs were pressed together, Brett's thigh still pushed against mine, sending all sorts of shivers through me.

Lizzy nudged my shoulder with hers. When I glanced at her, she waggled her brows, "So the city girl has some moves."

"Moves?" Mortification rushed through my veins.

The spunky redhead snickered before she elbowed me, "Girl, your swaying hips drew the attention of almost every available man in there last night."

Beside me, Brett let out a strangled groan which he covered up with a cough. I glanced over at him, there was so much heat burning in his eyes, I just about turned into a puddle of want. My mind drifted to a specific moment in the past. It was the first and last time Brett took me to a club. We hadn't even made it home before we clawed at each other, desperately seeking a release.

That was also the first time we'd made love in public, although, it wasn't the last time. I wondered if he remembered that night as vividly as I did.

"How are you feeling today?" Harper's voice pulled me from my lust-filled memories.

Immediately, my cheeks heated. Not only did I have no clue what I'd done at the bar, but I also had this sneaky suspicion that everyone knew where my thoughts had just gone. "A little fragile," I confessed.

She laughed. "We've all been there. Those cocktails are delicious, but they creep up on you with a vengeance."

"I guess I'm a bit of a lightweight."

Everyone laughed except Logan and Brett. They shared a look before Logan turned his attention to me. "Good news," he declared. "The parts we needed arrived this morning." The way he studied me made me feel uncomfortable. "You should be on your way before the day is out."

"That's great." I hoped that the disappointment flooding through me wasn't evident in my voice.

I felt Brett tense up next to me, and a small—okay, a huge— part of me hoped it was because he didn't want me to leave just yet.

"For there to be any truth to Logan's statement, I'd better go and finish up," he remarked, and then he completely knocked the breath out of me when he squeezed my leg. My head whipped to the side, and the pleading look in his eyes set fire to my soul. I swallowed hard to keep the gasp from slipping from my throat.

The warmth from his palm seeped through my clothes and skin, and sent white-hot need pulsing through me. I wanted to run my hands through his hair and feel the scrape of his whiskers against my skin. Every cell in my body begged to be fused with his.

The seconds ticked away, and I was vaguely aware of movement around the table, but I was unable to tear my gaze away from Brett's. I wasn't even sure he realized that his hand was gliding up my leg. Something had shifted between us, I had no idea what it was or why. If it weren't for the fact that I was still very conscious of the surrounding people, I would have leaned forward and kissed him until that pained look was replaced with something else.

Logan slapped him on the back, and the sound jolted us both out of the apparent spell we were under. "I thought we were leaving?"

Brett looked from me to Logan then back to me again, it appeared as if he was going to say something, but then he shook his head and slid out of the booth. "We are." Without so much as a backward glance, he stalked off, Logan close behind. I sat there gaping at his retreating back while my body yelled at him to come back.

"Uh, guess that's my cue, too." Chase also extracted himself from the booth and placed a hand on my shoulder. "It was great meeting you, Kenzie. Come say goodbye before you leave."

I was too flabbergasted to say anything else but, "Sure."

As soon as he was gone, Lizzy and Harper scooted closer and huddled together. It reminded me so much of high school when the girls couldn't wait to share the latest gossip.

Lizzy nudged me again, "So what's the deal with you and Brett?" Before I even had time to answer, she waved her index finger in front of me, "And don't even try to deny it—" she leaned closer and whisper-shouted, "—we've seen the looks."

I couldn't help but laugh. Lizzy reminded me so much of Zoe, I was sure if the two of them were to meet up, trouble would not be far behind. After I swallowed down some water, I cleared my throat. "We dated a long time ago."

"That much we know," Harper said. "What we're really interested in is why you're not dating anymore when there clearly is still so much chemistry between the pair of you?"

My gaze flitted between the two women. It was the strangest thing, I hardly knew them and yet I felt completely at ease with them. However, if Brett hadn't told the people he considered friends what had happened, I wasn't going to, either.

"It's complicated."

Lizzy placed her hand on my arm, "Oh sweetie, isn't everything? Just ask Harper."

Harper pulled her pink milkshake closer and slurped on it while nodding. "It's true," she said. "Falling in love with your neighbor while you're hiding from your abusive husband, now that's complicated."

I gaped at her like a fish out of water. How did I respond to that? Luckily, I didn't have to because she continued, "You don't have to tell us, or anyone for that matter. But know this, not even *complicated* can stand in fate's way."

"Sorry to interrupt." I turned my head, Lola was standing at the edge of our table. Lizzy and Harper's demeanors went from laid-back to defensive within a second. Both of them leaned their folded arms on the table and stared at Lola.

"Can I apologize?"

"That's a start." Lizzy announced before Harper bumped her with her elbow to which she let out a yelp and a "What?"

Lola nodded her head. "Look Kenzie," at the sound of my name I sat up straighter. "I'm not proud of it, and I really am sorry, but I'm the reason you were out of it last night."

"You are?" I sounded as confused as I felt.

"Yeah," Lola scratched the back of her neck, and I could tell she had difficulty making eye contact with me. "I…um…spiked your cocktails."

I felt violated. "Why would you do that?"

"Because I was being petty and childish."

Honestly, I didn't know what to think. On the one hand, I felt so incredibly violated, on the other, that thing that she did finally had Brett and me talking which led to a whole lot of realizations for me.

I should be angry, furious in fact, I just couldn't muster up anything other than gratitude.

Maybe there was something in the water that had twisted my wires, or maybe it was a certain hazel-eyed mechanic that had robbed me of my ability to think straight.

KENZIE

I WASN'T READY.

It was with a very heavy heart that I walked into the auto shop to collect my Mazda. *Would it be rude to leave and only come back tomorrow?* The thought hadn't even fully formed before I turned.

"You're here."

Logan's voice stopped me mid-step, and I bit back a curse. Planting a smile on my face, I pivoted to face him. "I am." As subtle as I could, I scanned the area, hoping to catch Brett.

"He already left."

"I'm sorry?" I feigned ignorance. "Who left?"

One of those laughs that came straight from the belly filled the air. "Ah, come on now…"

I huffed out a breath and spread my arms wide, "Fine. I wanted to say goodbye in person."

Logan motioned for me to follow him up the stairs that led to an office. Once he moved behind the desk, he pulled an envelope from the top drawer. My heart stopped beating as he held it out to me. If it was another letter from Brett, I didn't want it.

With a frown, he shook the brown manila, "Your invoice and key fob."

"Right." I snatched the envelope from him and removed its contents. While my eyes scanned over the paper, my brain was somewhere else. I didn't care how long it took, but I wasn't leaving Willow Creek until I got some answers from Brett.

"Can I ask you a favor?" Along with my question, I handed Logan my credit card.

He didn't hide his smile as he reached for the tiny machine on his desk and swiped my card. "'Course."

"I'm absolutely horrible with directions," I admitted. "Will you please draw me a map to the cabin?" Being as secluded as it was, I doubted that the address for Brett's cabin would be listed on any application.

With a nod of his head, he grabbed a pen and a piece of paper and started scribbling. When he was done, he held it out to me but didn't let go. "I'm not a person who meddles," he insisted. "Brett is family, and I look out for family." I blinked and tipped my head. "Now, I don't know exactly how things went down with you two, but I remember how it affected him, how it *still* affects him. You be mindful of that when you go out there."

With my spine straightened, I held his stare until he relinquished his hold on the scrap of paper. "Thank you." With a lot of care, I folded the map in half and slid it into my back pocket.

As if the last few minutes never happened, Logan proceeded to explain all the work that had been done on my car, and after I signed the job card, I was on my way.

Back at the guesthouse, I stared at the clothes laid out on the bed. On one side was, what used to be, my favorite business suit. Dean had always complimented me on how well the navy brought out my eyes. Next to the suit was a pair of faded jeans with a plain white t-shirt.

To most people that would just be two outfits beside each other. To me, it was two very different people sprawled out on the bed, and I had to decide which one was the real me.

Instead of deciding that instant, I made my escape to the bathroom where I took a shower. A shower that lasted so long, the water had turned cold. With my hands planted on my hips, I returned to the bed, my gaze bouncing between the outfits.

I reached for the jeans and t-shirt, and a slow smile spread across my face. Every item I donned brought with it a new sense of freedom and finally being in control. When my bags were packed, I went in search of Mrs. Davis.

I found her sitting in the garden. "May I?"

Happiness twinkled in her eyes as she patted the empty space next to her, "Please." We sat in silence for a couple of minutes, admiring her beautiful garden. A pair of butterflies fluttered past, and my heart pinched.

"Are you heading home, dear?"

I wanted to tell her that I wasn't going home, I was returning to the place where my belongings were. Right then, I didn't know where home was. Instead, I whispered, "Yes."

Mrs. Davis's elderly hand covered mine, "And you're sure you're not leaving anything behind?"

My gaze snapped to hers, and I was certain she saw the question burning in my eyes. She smiled a smile that said I still needed to learn everything she'd already forgotten about life. "I'm afraid there are a lot of things I'm not sure of, Mrs. Davis."

"As long as you leave with no regrets." She gave my hands a quick squeeze and slowly pushed to her feet. "I'm not saying goodbye," she winked at me and then strolled in the direction of the house.

A few minutes later I was behind the wheel of my Mazda, heading down a dirt road wondering if I'd completely lost my mind. I felt relieved when I pulled up in front of the cabin and spotted Brett's parked truck.

Relief soon made way for nerves when I approached the door. I raised my hand to knock but stopped when I heard faint hammering. Curiosity got the better of me, and I set off to inspect where the sound came from.

I had no idea what I was expecting to find, but it definitely was not Brett standing in front of a massive blowtorch tinkering with something attached to a metal rod. The workshop looked like it could have been a barn at some point — if barns consisted of cement walls and steel doors.

I couldn't make out all the equipment in there, but some of the stuff looked familiar. Just before everything between Brett and I went south, he'd started looking into glass blowing. He'd spent hours and hours browsing through sites looking for the equipment he needed.

Judging by the three benches, two of them containing torches, and the array of contraptions around him, he'd found everything he'd been looking for.

He was so lost in what he was doing; I took the time to shamelessly ogle him. I'd always rolled my eyes at the parts in romance novels where the heroine just looked at the guy, and she turned to mush.

Until I met Brett Carter.

One look from him and my pulse was on fire, one lop-sided grin and my entire body turned into a furnace.

Still unaware of my presence, he balanced the rod on the bench before him and gripped the hem of his shirt to wipe the sweat from his face.

And, holy moly, I just about melted into a puddle when I was given an eyeful of his perfectly sculpted abs and that delectable V that disappeared into his low-slung jeans. I gulped down some much-needed air and chewed on my lip.

The man was all kinds of fine wrapped up in a package good enough to eat.

He paused mid-wipe and our gazes collided. My feet began to move and didn't stop until I was just a few inches from him. He let go of the shirt and took me in, in an agonizingly slow perusal. I felt every cell in my body come alive under his gaze.

"I thought you left?"

Tilting my chin and squaring my shoulders, I said, "You and I have unfinished business."

He raised an eyebrow. "Oh?" His eyes dropped to my mouth and then lower before returning to mine, unmasked heat simmering in them.

"Can we talk?" How I managed to ignore the tug low in my belly, and the warmth spreading through me, was anyone's guess.

Brett sobered in an instant and nodded. "We'll head inside in a minute." He then turned off the blowtorch and flicked a few switches.

"You're not going to close it?" I asked when he started for the cabin without shutting the doors to his workshop.

He glanced over his shoulder and shrugged, "No one here but us, Sweet—" the endearment died on his tongue, and he continued his trek inside. I took a fortifying breath and followed him.

"You wanted to talk, so talk," he spat as soon as I entered. His walls were back up, and I doubted whether I'd be able to break through them.

Still, I was going to try.

"I never had the chance to tell you this," I began. "Those pills, I only used them to help me study. You know how my dad was, and if I didn't get good grades, he would have disowned me. Although, in hindsight that wouldn't have been such a bad thing."

I shook my head and continued, "I wasn't some strung out druggie. College was harder than I thought it would be and I needed a little help."

"You should have told me."

A sardonic laugh bubbled up. "Yeah, you're probably right. I just loved you so much; I couldn't bear for you to look at me differently."

"Kenzie—"

"Why did you never reply to any of my letters?" I finally voiced the one question I needed an answer to most of all.

Deep frown lines creased his forehead, and even from where I was standing I could see he was biting down on his teeth. "What do you mean?" I barely heard the words through his clenched jaw.

I swallowed to ease the dryness in my throat. "I wrote to you every day," I cried. "Explaining how my dad had kept me from going to see you. I couldn't even make it past the gate, Brett!" I took a step forward. "But not once did you write back."

Gone were all my good intentions, I was angry too and, yeah, I hadn't made the right decisions but neither did he.

"You accused me of not having the decency to tell you things to your face, but all you did was lash out at me." My voice was rising. "You—" I stabbed my index finger in his direction. "— were no better than me."

He looked as if I had just slapped him across the face. "You wrote to me?"

"Every day, for almost seven months." I didn't understand the confusion flashing in his eyes.

His gaze dropped to the floor, a quizzical expression pulling his brows together. "You didn't get any of my letters?"

"The only letter I got from you was the one where you told me that you wished you'd never met me," I mumbled.

Brett shook his head vehemently and rushed toward me. "You don't understand, Kenzie, I sent letters before that one. I tried calling your house, but your mom would never let me talk to you."

"You did?"

He cupped my shoulders and stooped, eyes full of concern scanning over me. "Sweetheart, before I went away you were my whole world. That wasn't about to change because I traded my apartment for a six by nine cell."

"But you said—"

"Those words were written in anger. You never showed up when you said you would. I was hurting—" he touched his chest, "—here."

Never in my life had I felt as confused as I did at that moment. "I don't understand," my gaze shifted to the side for a moment then snapped back to his. "You called the house?"

He swallowed, "I did."

My hands flew to my mouth, and I took a step back. "No," I breathed. "This can't be right."

"Kenzie?" Brett's voice was filled with so much tenderness; I wanted to wrap it around me like a safety blanket.

"Don't you see? My dad had found a way to intercept our letters. I should have paid more attention when he'd vowed he'd make sure we'd never see each other again." I took another step back. "I'm so stupid."

As the heart-shattering realization dawned, angry tears slipped from my eyes. How was it possible for parents to put their child through so much hurt?

BRETT

I HELD MY BREATH AS I WATCHED THE EMOTIONS FLIT ACROSS KENZIE'S FACE. She shook her head and pressed a palm to her chest. "How could they do that?" The question slipped from her lips in a whisper.

"I don't know, Sweetheart." My answer barely registered as her gaze bounced from one place to the next. The tears rolling down her cheeks might as well have been my own. I felt her sadness in my bones.

For the short period, I'd had them, my parents had been the best two people I'd known. They'd both been artists. Momma was a very gifted painter, and there was not one sculptor as great as my dad. My parents were the reason I'd studied art. Unfortunately, an icy road had taken them from me far too soon. But in the end, I was thankful that they went together because the one would not have survived without the other.

I'd always believed that all kids were raised with the same amount of love and understanding I had been. I was proven wrong when I'd met Mr. and Mrs. Michaels for the first time. They'd had everything they could have possibly wanted, and it wasn't enough. Their daughter wasn't enough. Too many times I'd heard them tell her that she needed to remember who she was representing. That they had a reputation she had to uphold.

I'd kept my mouth shut for Kenzie.

Her parents and I had never really gotten along, but I respected them for raising such an incredible daughter. In this moment, though, I felt nothing but contempt for them. Anger, sadness, and, confusion all fought their way to the surface, and I honestly had no clue what to do.

I was torn between pulling her into my arms and beating the shit out of her daddy. That idiot had cost me—*us*—everything.

The more I thought about it, the more I realized that I should have figured out that her dad had kept her away. Kenzie had always told me about how influential the man had been. The thing was, when you're hurting you're incapable of thinking straight and more often than not, you want someone else to hurt with you.

Bile rose in my throat as I recalled the insults I'd thrown at Kenzie. I'd been an insensitive jerk—and that was putting it mildly. Throwing around words like *self-centered, spoiled little rich girl…* That familiar sense of panic started working its way through my veins again. With Kenzie in the state she was, there was no way I was going to leave her to run it out of my system.

But I did need to take the edge off.

I spun around and stalked to the kitchen where I pulled a beer from the fridge and gulped down half of it in one go. Kenzie's hesitant footfalls alerted me to her presence. Facing her, I swiped a palm over my beard and held the brew out to her.

With a small shake of her head, she leaned against the counter and crossed her arms in front of her.

Now was not the time to be drinking in her beauty but I couldn't help myself. I'd had need coursing through my veins the moment I'd spotted her standing outside my workshop.

There was no doubt that she'd rocked her pencil skirt and blouse when she'd arrived in town, but, Kenzie Michaels in a pair of tight fitting Levi's and a tee was enough to give any man fever dreams in broad daylight.

I brought the bottle back to my lips, hoping the cold brew would douse the flame of want raging inside me.

"Was it hard?" Kenzie raked her fingers through her hair before tucking a few strands behind her ear.

It is now. "What?" I heard the strain in my own voice.

"Prison?"

I glanced at the window and then back at her. After a deep breath, I spoke, "I'm not gonna lie, it was. Throw a bunch of men together under normal circumstances, and they're bound to have a pissing contest so you can imagine how much worse it is when we're all living like caged animals." Jail wasn't for wimps. However, Kenzie didn't need to know all the awful things I'd seen in there. I wasn't afraid to admit that there were times where I was scared shitless.

"Brett, I'm so sorry." Was I a bastard for loving the way the blue in her eyes turned a shade darker or how they couldn't hide what she was feeling?

"It wasn't all bad," I reassured her with a smile. "I'd met Logan while I was inside, and once I got out, he'd offered me a job at the shop."

Kenzie looked to the side, and I saw her throat work down a swallow. I had no doubt that it was tears she was pushing back. "I can tell that you're a close-knit bunch."

I resisted the urge to go to her. "They're my family."

She covered her face with both her hands. "We lost so much." It was barely a whisper. "I should have known that you'd never just throw me away like that." Those baby blues were trained on me again. "You probably think I'm stupid for not realizing it was all my parents' doing." Her voice was soft and filled with so much self-doubt; it made my heart ache.

Without giving it a second thought, I crossed the room. When I stood before her, I placed my finger under her chin and tilted her head up. She kept those big eyes of hers on me, rendering me helpless to look away. "I think you are a lot of things—" I finally rasped out. "—but stupid ain't one of 'em, Sweetheart."

Her lips lifted into a dry smile. "Right." She sounded as unconvinced as she looked, and so help me, I had no other choice than to lower my mouth to hers.

My lids wanted to close at the contact, but I forced them to stay open so I could see Kenzie's reaction. She went rigid, and those eyes of hers widened to their max. I was sure she was either going to shove me or slap me.

She didn't do either.

I felt her little sigh right before her body melted into mine, and she wound her arms around my neck. A groan rumbled its way through my chest as I gave into the heaviness of my lids.

Kenzie toyed with the ends of my hair; I deepened the kiss by plunging my tongue into her mouth. I'd wanted the kiss to be sweet and romantic but years of pent-up *everything* had me devouring her like the ravenous beast I was.

It was one of those breath-stealing, teeth-scraping kisses that almost verged on the edge of being painful. I dragged my right palm up her spine before I tangled my fingers into her hair, my left hand pressed hard into the small of her back, mashing our bodies even closer together.

With her pushed up against the counter and our bodies not even a breath apart; there was no hiding what I felt or what I *needed*. Kenzie dragged her knee along my outer thigh and rolled her hips against me; I damn near lost my mind. The needy whimpering coming from her had me grinding my hips in time with hers. I slid my hands over her ribs, brushing the sides of her breasts.

I abandoned her mouth in favor of the delicate skin below her ear. Kenzie's head fell back, and her hands slid to my biceps, her slender fingers biting into my skin. We were moving as if there were no clothes between us and I had no doubt that a few more of those intense movements would have us both done for.

My hands moved to her waist, and before she could even protest, I lifted her and parked her ass on the countertop.

Without breaking contact, I stepped between her parted thighs and kissed her with determination. Her tongue lapped and coiled, matching my every stroke with equal eagerness. She tasted of shattered dreams topped with a sprinkling of hope.

My hands slid up her legs, and my mind went to that butterfly on her skin. All I could think of doing was brushing my fingers over its intricate lines while my mouth teased the very core of her.

I didn't just want more of Kenzie, I wanted *all* of her.

Everything standing between us had to go, starting with her shirt. I yanked it over her head and threw it to the side. An animalistic growl, I hardly recognized, pushed from my lungs the moment my hands touched her bare skin.

Kenzie reached between us and tugged on my hem, soon my tee joined hers on the floor. Her delicate fingers brushed over my skin in an agonizingly slow way. Dragging her mouth away from mine, her head stooped, and she pressed her lips against the ink on my chest. Her breath was warm and her kisses achingly soft.

I completely lost it, shoving my hands into her hair and pulling her face back to mine. I didn't think I could kiss her with any more urgency or hunger, but I stood corrected as I took possession of her mouth once more.

Yearning to taste more of her, my lips slid down her throat only pausing to press my tongue against her racing pulse. I took a breath and with it sent her familiar flowery scent straight to my lungs.

I ventured farther, scraping my teeth over her collarbone and loving on that sensitive spot where her neck and shoulder joined. Kenzie's back arched and I nipped at the exposed skin at the swell of her breast. When I pulled her hips flush against mine, her gasp turned into a moan, and dammit, it was the sexiest sound.

My mouth moved lower and lower, kissing and nipping just above the waistband of her jeans.

I didn't expect the soft pop of her button to be as sobering as it was.

What the hell am I doing? My gaze traveled over her body, taking in every little detail. Her chest was heaving. The vein in her neck jumping. Her swollen lips were somewhere between red and pink, and it was the prettiest sight.

I could have her right there on the counter in my kitchen. I could get lost in the warmth of her body and drive us both to the brink of ecstasy. But that wasn't what I wanted.

I didn't want to screw Kenzie, I wanted to *make love* to her.

Moving up her body again, I cupped her cheeks and pressed a kiss to the tip of her nose. With a sigh, I dropped my forehead to hers. "Sweetheart, don't go home to him tonight, stay with me."

Chapter 20

KENZIE

REALITY REACHED OUT AND WRAPPED ITS COLD FINGERS AROUND MY THROAT BEFORE SQUEEZING. A bucket of ice over the head would have been less sobering than Brett's words. I pulled his hands from my face and held them in mine.

"You have no idea how much I want to," The heat of his touch still lingered, and I desperately needed him to do something about the throbbing ache still pulsing through me. But it would be wrong to have Brett make love to me under these circumstances. I swallowed down the cactus-like lump and sucked in a breath. "I can't."

Brett's gaze snapped to mine and all the hurt and confusion I saw in them lacerated my heart. He snatched his hands out of my grasp and started pacing. "Am I missing something here?" I knew the anger in his voice came from a place of deep-rooted pain. "A moment ago you had no reservations. You seemed perfectly fine with me having my way with you."

A moment ago I was caught up in a lust-bubble where reality didn't exist. His gaze momentarily dropped to my chest, and I was reminded of my state of undress. I slid off the counter and picked up my shirt.

"I need to sort things out with Dean," I pulled the cotton over my head and dragged my fingers through my tangled tresses.

Brett planted his hands on his hips and glared at me. "Was this your plan all along?" When I just stared at him, his rant continued, "You come here, looking like *that*—" his hand swept over my body before returning to his hip. "—let me touch you, taste you and then turn around and tell me I can never have you."

I felt my own anger start to simmer to a boil. "It's not like that, and you know it."

"Apparently I don't know shit anymore."

Instead of acting like the lady my mother had raised, I stomped over to him and shoved his chest, hard. "Damn you, Brett!" Another shove. "When I'm with you I don't want anything between us, especially not guilt." My brows pulled together, and my tone softened. "Dean is a good man, he doesn't deserve this."

I thought understanding would dawn, I was sorely mistaken. The anger I'd just seen reached a new height when he roared,

"What about what *I* deserve?" His breaths came in quick spurts, almost as if he was gasping for air. I reached out for him, but the ice in his stare had my arms dropping to my sides.

"You need to leave," he finally gritted out. "Get in your car and go back to your perfect little life where there is no space for someone like me."

All the anger I felt was replaced with sadness. "You're not even listening to me." With a shake of my head, I turned around and headed for the door. I took five steps and then glanced over my shoulder at the man still seething, the man I so desperately loved. "You need to stop living in the past, Brett; the future is passing you by."

I straightened my spine and walked out of his cabin with my head held high. He made no move to stop me, not that I thought he would. It was only when I couldn't see Willow Creek in my rearview mirror anymore that I allowed the tears to roll down my cheeks.

BRETT

THE SOUND OF GRAVEL CRUNCHING BENEATH TIRES might as well have been a punch to the gut or a knife to my heart. I raced to the door and was just in time to see Kenzie's Mazda kick up a cloud of dust as she sped away.

"Shit!" I yelled and as I headed back inside the curses didn't stop coming. What the hell was wrong with me? Stomping into the kitchen, I tried to replay the conversation we'd had mere moments ago but to be honest, I didn't remember much past, *'Dean is a good man, he doesn't deserve this.'*

I both envied and hated the bastard. Somewhere in my brain, it registered that neither Kenzie nor I was to blame for what happened between us all those years ago. That didn't stop the feeling of betrayal or pang of jealousy eating at my gut. Dean, the asshole, had Kenzie's loyalty and her love too.

I looked down at my hands; I could still feel the smoothness of her skin. The taste of her still lingered on my tongue, and her scent filled my lungs with every breath I took.

My discarded beer caught my eye, and I moved to grab it, only it was empty. The volcano of anger inside me finally erupted as I hurled the bottle across the room. The shattering sound of glass barely registered.

Fueled by anger and high on hurt, I marched into the living room. As usual, the butterflies on the bookcase mocked me. They had no right to the space they were taking up, in my home and my heart.

I crossed the room, and with one swipe of my arm, I sent the delicate sculptures flying through the air. What was left of me broke into pieces right alongside them. One question remained as I sank to the floor.

Why is it so easy for her to leave me behind?

I was nervous and excited, but mostly nervous. Except for that brief time in court, I hadn't seen Kenzie in months. I had been writing to her like a fiend, sometimes twice a day because we never knew which one of the letters actually made it out.

Although she had yet to respond to any of my mail, I received word from one of the guards that I would be getting a visitor. These days were the absolute worst for me. It was tough to see that even the most horrendous criminals had someone who came to see them, while I had no one.

I could still remember that very first day, the anticipation of seeing Kenzie again had excitement bursting from my pores. Instead of my girl showing up, it was Axil sitting there. He didn't even need to say the words, I'd already known it was the first and last time I was going to see him.

Apparently, his reputation meant more than our friendship did.

For weeks after that, I'd waited and waited, but, no one else came to visit. I'd even had a few run-ins with the guards because I believed that they weren't sending out my letters to Kenzie.

But none of that mattered now, 'cause today I was finally going to see my girl.

"You keep on going back and forth like that, you're gonna dig us a hole outta here." My cellmate, Logan quipped from where he was perched on the top bunk. "Hey man," he said when I didn't answer him. "She's gonna show."

If there ever was a silver lining to ending up in this hell hole, it was Logan. When I'd arrived, he was already six months into a three-year sentence. We'd become fast friends, and in a place like this, you needed all the friends you could get.

Still, I hadn't gone into detail over Kenzie, he just knew I had a girl on the outside and that it was serious for me.

The guard sauntered up to our cell, Cheshire cat grin in place. "Jackson," he called to Logan. "You have visitors." Every Saturday, without fail, his family showed up. It was the only time I envied him. Turning to me, the guard's smile turned sinister, "No one for you, yet, Carter."

My friend jumped off the bed and smacked my shoulder blade twice as he walked past me. Again, he repeated, "She's gonna show."

How wrong he'd been.

Visiting hours had come and gone and no Kenzie. My already lacerated heart took its final beating then. Reaching under my pillow, I pulled out the notepad and vowed to myself that that was the last letter I'd ever write to Kenzie Michaels.

Breathe.

I need to breathe. My head swiveled from side to side, and I swore I could see her everywhere. Standing in my doorway, wearing my shirt. Nibbling on the corner of her mouth while she pushed her hair behind her ear. Running her tongue over her lip right before she pressed her lips to mine.

"Shit!!" I cursed again.

After years and years of carefully guarding what was left of my heart, I'd dropped the ball, and it had been detrimental.

Bringing my hand up, I rubbed at my chest already knowing that nothing would soothe the ache inside. My gaze dropped to the mess surrounding me, and I caught sight of one little butterfly still intact. I reached forward to scoop it up.

Pushing to my feet, I returned it to its spot on my bookcase. Gently I brushed over its delicate blue wings, embracing the sting of betrayal and absolute devastation that I knew was coming.

KENZIE

I STOOD IN THE DOORWAY OF MY APARTMENT, WAITING FOR THAT RELIEF AT BEING HOME TO SETTLE INTO MY BONES.

It never came.

With a heavy sigh, I closed the door behind me, and after locking it, I threw my keys into the butterfly-shaped bowl that sat on the table next to the door. My heart constricted, and fresh tears filled my eyes.

My mind immediately went to Brett and how long it must've taken him to make all those tiny butterflies. The time and effort he'd spent on every little detail.

Brett.

I brushed the hot tears away, wishing it was as easy to wipe his image from my brain. Oh, how I'd hoped that that kiss would have been the start to our new beginning, our chance to reclaim what was stolen from us.

Why didn't he understand that I needed to do this? How could I have shared his bed when technically I was still another man's girlfriend? It didn't matter that Brett owned me, heart and soul, I still had to do what was right.

I pressed my palm between my breasts and begged for the ache to go away. Even just for a couple of minutes. *"Please?"*

In a dreamlike state, I moved from the spacious living area into the kitchen. Like a zombie, I pulled a mug from the cupboard along with a chamomile tea bag. I started to fill the little kettle that sat atop my stove with water and stopped short.

The little window above my sink suddenly turned into a screen and rolling images of my short time in Willow Creek played out like a movie in front of me. Brett Carter front and center in every single frame. That very first ice-filled look. The determined way he'd marched up to me in the bar. My hands splayed on his chest. The way he'd cupped my cheeks and then finally the look in his hazel eyes right before he kissed me.

"Stop!" The kettle fell from my hands, water splashing everywhere. Immediately my hands moved to my eyes to cover them. It didn't work. The images just kept coming over and over again.

As the pain in my chest reached breaking point, my knees gave out, and I slid to the floor, landing in a miserable heap. My body convulsed with every soul-shattering sob that left it. I'd never felt pain like that in my life before, and I doubted I ever would again for it was surely going to break me.

I cried for I didn't know how long, but when I was certain there were no more tears left in me, I sucked in a breath and pushed to my feet. My bathroom that was just down the hall suddenly felt miles away, and I didn't know if I had enough strength left in me to drag my tired body there.

When I finally stood under the warm spray of water, a little clarity came. I had questions for my parents. Boy, did I have questions. They needed to make me understand why they did what they did.

I pressed my forehead against the tiles and thought of Dean. The way I'd behaved wasn't right; he didn't deserve any of it. Was I a bad person because kissing Brett hadn't felt like cheating? It felt a hell of a lot like coming in from the cold and having the fire warm you to your very core.

"Ugh!" I shut off the water and snatched a towel from the rack. After wiping the fogginess from the mirror, I confronted my reflection. As much as I wanted to, I couldn't find it in me to belittle the woman I saw staring back at me.

She looked a little worse for wear but a whole lot lost.

It was time for me to take ownership of my life—mistakes and all.

A plan formed in my head as I padded to my room. I dropped the towel and pulled a pair of sleep shorts and a cami from my armoire. Brush in hand; I slipped onto the stool in front of my dressing table. The tiny box hiding behind my jewelry case caught my attention.

I pulled it from behind the impressive pewter box that'd been a gift from Dean. A sad smile tugged at my lips as I ran my fingers over the engraving on the worn wood.

Forever. Refusing to shed one more tear, I swallowed them down and lifted the lid. There weren't many keepsakes in there. A sugar packet from my first date with Brett, a butterfly that he drew for me, the same one sitting on my thigh, and then finally the letter.

With shaky fingers, I unfolded the piece of paper and braced for the shame and hurt that always accompanied the words.

Dear Kenzie.

Having your choices taken away from you brings a lot of things into focus.

Brings all your previous choices into focus.

I've had a lot of time to think about why I gave so much of my life to you. And honestly, no amount of time will ever give me the answer. I can't understand why I loved you. Why I trusted you?

Did you think I wouldn't figure it out? Did you think you could always hide your 'daddy's girl' facade?

Well, lucky for me I see you now. I know who you are. A lying fake, spoiled little rich girl that has no spine and even fewer morals. How convenient it must be that I'm locked away. That I took the fall for you. I hope Gregory keeps you warm. I hope he screws you into oblivion every night, so you get the rest I doubt your conscious will allow.

I hope you can live with yourself because I know I could never live with you in my life ever again.

I placed the letter on the table and waited. There was no shame. No hurt. What did come was determination. I was going to prove, even if it was just to myself, that I wasn't that weak, sheltered girl anymore.

The insecure girl that would do anything for her father's approval made way for a woman with nothing left to lose.

A knock on the front door had me frowning at my reflection. *What time is it?* I didn't even know. More banging, it sounded a bit more urgent this time. I grabbed my robe from behind the closet and moved to see who was pounding on the door.

With my hand on the handle, I peeked through the peephole. "Oh shoot," I muttered when Dean's face came into focus. I didn't have the strength for the conversation we needed to have, but I also knew he wasn't going anywhere until we had a face to face.

Tightening the robe around my waist, I pushed down on the handle and pulled it toward me. A second later, a very tired looking Dean stepped forward.

I took him in from head to toe. Blond hair, neatly cut and not a strand out of place. Piercing blue eyes that crinkled at the corners when he laughed. A strong clean-shaven jaw. My gaze traveled up and down his lean body. He wore a suit like it had been made for him—which it probably had. The white button-down beneath his black blazer pulled taut across his chest.

My tummy should be fluttering, and my pulse should be racing. It wasn't. My heart didn't sing like it did when Brett was in the vicinity. My body didn't scream *take me now*.

"You didn't tell me you were coming home today." He said by way of greeting. I waited for the sound of his voice to coat my insides with warmth, but it never came.

I shrugged, "I didn't know."

Something flashed across Dean's face, but I was too damn tired to figure out what it was. He leaned forward and for the life of me, I couldn't tell you why I did what I did. Just as his lips came within inches of mine, I twisted my face to the side.

To his credit, he didn't say anything although he did scan the little he could see of my apartment.

"Can I come in?"

The right thing would have been to invite him in, make coffee and talk things through like adults. That's what my mother would have expected of me. "Dean, I just got home a few minutes ago," the lie tasted bitter on my tongue. "I'm beyond exhausted."

His Adam's apple bobbed up and down with a tentative nod of his head. "Dinner, tomorrow?"

When I agreed, we said our goodbyes without so much as a hug. Leaning back against the closed door, I stared at my ceiling and asked for the strength I needed to get through the next couple of days.

BRETT

I ROLLED OUT FROM UNDER MR. HENDERSON'S OLD CHEV and wiped my hands on the rag hanging over the side-mirror. Catching a glimpse of my reflection in the window, I grimaced. I looked exactly how I felt.

Sleep had eluded me; every time I tried to close my eyes Kenzie's face mocked me. It might've been my imagination, but I could still smell her on my sheets. I dropped the old cloth and snatched my water from the bench. It was scorching out, and it was fitting considering I was living in my own version of hell.

My grip around the plastic tightened, and I tried to push aside the anger, which was trying to rise up. Logically, I knew I had no right to be angry with Kenzie. It had always been my decision to take the fall for her, and even with everything I knew now, I'd still do it again in a heartbeat.

You protected the ones you loved no matter what.

And I loved Kenzie with every cell in my body. Sure, I was angry, and my soul had taken a good beating, but that woman was the only one my heart would ever beat for. I'd realized a long time ago that I'd never be over her and the dead feeling inside of me was proof of that.

Like a caterpillar needed a cocoon to turn into a beautiful butterfly, I needed Kenzie to live.

I took a breath through my nose. It might've taken me years to get to a point where she wasn't my every thought, but I'd gotten there eventually, and I would get there again.

"Hey, man."

I glanced over my shoulder and spotted Eli coming toward me, thumbs hooked through his belt loops, his assessing gaze sweeping over the shop.

"What's up?" I greeted him with a lift of my chin.

The now familiar scowl on his face didn't faze me at all. I knew where it stemmed from and I sympathized. The guy had even worse luck than me when it came to love.

"Logan around?"

Leaning my hips against the bench, I crossed my ankles and folded my arms in front of me, "Nah, he went to pick up Dozer's food, but if you ask me he's over there kissing Harper silly in the kitchen."

Eli pulled a face, and something between a groan and a hum passed his lips. Not only was the guy not a fan of public displays of affection, but he was also still finding his way around Harper. They hadn't started off on the best foot. Being the suspicious guy that he was, Eli had completely misread her situation; it'd caused quite a stir between the brothers.

When he didn't leave, I asked, "Was there something you needed?"

He crossed his arms in front of him and widened his stance. With his head cocked to the side the way it was, I already knew what was coming. "So you know that Kenzie woman?"

I narrowed my eyes and hissed, "You know I know her, Chase gossips more than the old ladies at the hair salon."

Eli's lips twitched, which was about the closest thing to a smile the guy was willing to give. He cleared his throat, "Chase might've mentioned something, besides even a blind man could see the way you were undressing her with your eyes the other night." He pinched his nose, "I just don't need any more drama in my town. That thing with Harper's ex, had been enough."

I pushed off the bench and mirrored his stance. "What are you talking about?"

He raised an eyebrow, "If drinks are getting spiked, catfights are right behind it." His shoulders rose and fell in a shrug, "And she has a boyfriend. Dean Mathis, I believe is his name." Eli, the thorough Sheriff that he was, made a point of running background checks on every Willow Creek newcomer. I did say he was suspicious.

His words registered and the bastard's name had me clenching my jaw. "Yeah, well, I'm drama free, my friend. She left town last night."

Eli nodded, and relief softened his features a bit. "I hate to say this, but it's for the best, man. Girls like that ain't good for the old ticker, ya know."

Too bad she's the only one it beats for.

"So, are we seeing you on Friday?" He held up his hand, "And before you decline, momma wanted me to tell you that she's about to put your face on a milk carton."

I couldn't help but smile. When I'd started over in Willow Creek, Logan's family had treated me like one of their own. They'd given me so much; essentially I'd gained back the family I'd lost and then some. Most days, I felt like an ungrateful idiot 'cause I'd trade it all to be able to spend my life with Kenzie.

I needed to stop thinking like that, it wasn't going to happen. My happily ever after belonged to Dean-asshole-Mathis.

"I'll be there."

KENZIE

HAVING LUNCH WITH YOUR PARENTS SHOULDN'T BE NERVE-WRACKING. And yet, as I stood in front of the imposing white door, my nerves were hanging on by the tiniest of threads. I glanced down at my outfit and just knew the sparks were going to fly the moment Diana Michaels laid eyes on me.

With a deep breath, I wrapped my fingers around the heavy golden knocker and banged it down twice. Inside my chest, my heart was thumping to a frantic rhythm.

"Breathe," I whispered. "You can do this. You *have* to do this."

The door opened with a whoosh and I'd never been as happy to see Selma. 'Maid' was her job title, but she'd dried more of my tears than my mother had. I stooped and wrapped my arms around her plump body.

Her hands came to my face, and her smile widened. "Kenzie," she squealed. "Just look at you."

I straightened and dragged my fingers through my loose hair before running my palms down my jeans. "It's different, I know." According to my mother, a lady should only ever wear dresses or skirts, and her hair should be out of her face at all times.

"Well, I like it." Selma closed the door, and I followed her to the dining room. On our way there she updated me on how her children were doing. And as petty as it was, I found myself wishing that I'd been one of Selma and Eduardo's children.

She moved to pour me a glass of water, and I stopped her. "You know, you don't have to do that for me." I took the pitcher from her, and while I filled my glass, she patted my cheek. The sound of my mother's heels clicking against the pristine tiles drew closer. "You might want to stay out of the range of fire, Selma." I gave her an apologetic look. If things were going to go even half as bad as I suspected they would, the people employed by my parents were in for a tough day.

"I'm proud of you," Selma gushed before she hurried away. I drew strength from her words as the clicking became louder.

"Kenzie?"

My mother stopped abruptly, and her hand flew to her mouth while the other touched her hair.

"Hi, Mom." I pulled my shoulders to my ears and gave her a half-smile.

She shook her head as she approached me. The hands resting on my shoulders didn't feel as soft as Selma's embrace had, and the two pecks to my cheeks felt stiff.

"Your father will join us in a minute." She pulled out her chair and laid an unfolded napkin in her lap. Bringing her fingers up, she toyed with the string of pearls circling her neck. "Does Dean know you're back? The poor man was so worried about you."

I nodded, "He does, we're having dinner tonight."

Her hand slipped from her pearls and flattened against her chest. Relief rushed out of her in a quick breath. "Oh, that's good. You're not getting any younger, Kenzie. When I was your age your daddy and I already had you." She started talking faster, and I knew better than to interrupt. "Dean's mother and I went to lunch the other day—such a lovely lady, she is—we were thinking that a summer wedding would be perfect. And I saw this absolutely stunning Vera—"

"I'm breaking up with Dean, Mom." I deadpanned.

The color drained from my mother's face so fast, you'd think I just told her my grandma rose from the dead. Tiny squeaky sounds came from the back of her throat while she just stared at me with wide eyes.

Don't get me wrong, I loved my parents. They gave me a roof over my head, they fed me, and in their way, they showed me affection. Right at that moment though, all I saw was the lies they told for their own personal gain.

Weren't a mother, and a father supposed to love their child unconditionally?

"That's preposterous," my mother gasped when she finally found her voice.

"What's preposterous?" My father entered the dining room and, he too, stopped short when he spotted me. "Kenzie what on earth are you wearing?"

I didn't have time to utter a single word before my mother jumped up and pointed an accusatory finger at me. "She is having one of those nervous breakdowns, Walter. She just told me she's leaving Dean."

My father cupped my mother's shoulders, "Calm down, Diana, she'll do no such thing."

The anger that had been simmering just below the surface finally came to a boil. "It's going to happen, Daddy and there's nothing you can do to stop me."

My father's eyes cut to me. "Watch your tone, young lady."

I shook my head, "Why does it matter who I date, anyway?"

"It matters because we have a reputation to uphold—" I rolled my eyes and then looked away while my dad went on. "—Dean comes from the same background as you do, he shares our values, and he does not want you for financial gain."

My gaze snapped to his lightning fast, "Not like Brett Carter had, right Daddy?"

My father puffed out his chest and gave my mother's shoulder a squeeze. I wondered if they'd been waiting for this conversation for years. When Brett was sentenced, my dad had forbidden me to go see him. I wasn't even allowed to mention his name in their presence. In their minds, my relationship with Brett never happened.

"Funny how things work out sometimes," I went on. "How strange and wonderful that the town I get stuck in turned out to be his town." My father's jaw muscles started jumping, and my mother couldn't even look at me. "Brett and I had a nice long chat, and you wouldn't believe the things we learned."

"Kensington June Michaels, now you listen here—"

Swallowing the urge to lower my eyes and shrink back at my father's tone, I took a step forward, "No, Daddy, you listen. I don't know how you did it, but I know what you did." Tears stung the back of my eyes, but I forced them away. "Why? Did you even care that he made me happy? Do you even know that he took the fall *for me*?"

My mother's gasp filled the room, but it was my father's jaw that ticked faster that send me reeling. "You knew?" I dragged

my fingers through my hair, "You knew and said nothing?" Turning my gaze to the window, I almost laughed at the perfect picture outside. Everything from the well-manicured lawn to the tennis court that no one used was just for show. Just to keep up appearances. My gaze snapped back to my parents, my fury finally reaching its pinnacle.

"He only did that to protect me from having to tell you that your perfect daughter isn't so perfect." My voice screeched through the room. "You kept me from seeing him even when you knew he was innocent!"

"What is she talking about, Walter?"

My father gave me a look that said he'd deal with me in a minute before he turned to my mother, "Nothing Diana, let me talk to Kenzie alone." Ever the perfect wife, my mother nodded and left the room without even looking at me.

"Now you listen here—" my father roared as soon as his wife was out of earshot. "—I only did what was best for you. That boy would have ended up behind bars, anyway. Kids like that always do?"

I threw my hands in the air in disbelief, "Kids like that? Are you even listening to yourself?" Shaking my head, I continued, "Did you know that *that boy* happened to ace all his classes while I was struggling to maintain a B-grade, which I only achieved by using drugs, I might add!"

My father slammed his closed fists against the table, and I startled. In all my life I had never seen him lose control like that, but I was determined that it would not intimidate me. "I only did what was best for you!" My dad's voice reverberated off the walls.

"And being miserable is what's best for me?"

Running a palm down his tie, he calmly stated, "I did what I had to do, and when you and Dean walk down the aisle, you'll thank me."

"Are you nuts?" To be fair, the way I was yelling made me sound like the crazy person in the room. I just couldn't help it.

"Kenzie—"

I held up both my hands, "You know what? I'm done, Daddy. No more Dean and no more working for you either. I quit."

Shaky legs carried me to my car. I slid behind the wheel thinking that was both the bravest and scariest thing I'd ever done.

BRETT

I FELT A LITTLE GUILTY AS I MADE MY WAY DOWN THE DIRT ROAD leading to the Jackson ranch. It had been a long while since I'd visited. Instead of spending time with the people who were like family to me, I'd been keeping my bed warm with any willing woman.

Easing my foot off the gas, I slowed enough so that I could properly appreciate the scenery. I'd always loved how the trees bowing over the road created an arch with soft rays of light filtering through the leaves. Out in the distance, I caught sight of Chris, the Jackson's ranch manager, tending to a few of the horses.

It had always baffled me why not one of the brothers had stayed on at the ranch. All three of them would jump in and help in a heartbeat if it was required though. Even I had been roped in to help mend a fence a time or two. I guess what it ultimately boiled down to was the need to have your own identity.

One thing was for sure, Charles and Daisy Jackson did not begrudge any of their sons that, in fact, they encouraged them to be who they wanted to be. I slowed down even more, my gaze leisurely gliding over the impressive land. Mr. Jackson had offered to sell me a good chunk of it, but at the time all I'd wanted was solitude. I had needed a place for my workshop and the space to run free.

I rolled past the pen and Chris greeted me with a lift of his Stetson, behind him I spotted a newcomer to the ranch. With a slight tilt of my head, I greeted him too. Once my truck was parked behind Logan's, I made my way to the door stopping briefly to look at the barn. Its bright yellow paint never failed to put a smile on my face.

Before I even managed a knock, the door flew open and Mrs. Jackson assaulted me with affection. My arms were pinned to my sides so I couldn't return her embrace. But, man, it felt good. Her hugs were laced with the type of comfort you only get from a mother. The kind that said: *I know you're dealing with stuff, but everything will be okay*.

Clearing my throat to rid myself of the lump forming there, I gruffly said, "It's good to see you too, Mrs. J." Much to her irritation, I refused to call her by her first name, I had way too much respect for the woman.

She released her death-grip on me and cupped my face in her hands. "It's been too long, Brett. We've missed you." The sincerity in her eyes had me swallowing down another lump.

"I know, I'm sorry."

A smile so wide, the Cheshire cat would envy it, spread across her face; the corners of her eyes wrinkling up. "No matter, you're here now."

"Brett!!" Over Mrs. Jackson's shoulder, I caught sight of Molly and Flynn barreling toward me. I dropped to my haunches and held both my palms up to them. Squeals of delight accompanied their high-fives.

"You two behaving?" Molly snickered, and mischief sparkled in Flynn's eyes. With a wink, I smiled and stated, "You make me proud."

When I pushed to my feet, I was met with Mrs. Jackson's narrowed eyes. "I can't wait for your babies, I'm gonna teach them to be so naughty." Mirth sparkled in her eyes while a cinder block landed on my chest.

Kids of my own had never been a thought. Don't get me wrong, I adored my friends' children, and I would protect them like they were my blood. But before I could even think about having kids, I needed to find a woman who I wanted to spend my life with. The sad fact was the only woman who fit that bill was miles away pledging her undying love to another man.

"C'mon," my surrogate mother slipped her arm through mine, and we walked through the house to the backyard. It never ceased to amaze me how much this house felt like home to me. I was disappointed in myself for neglecting the important people in my life.

As we stepped outside, Mrs. Jackson halted me. The kids stormed ahead, and once they were out of earshot, she turned to me. "Over the years, you've become like a son to me." Her eyes scanned over my face, the love in them warming me. "And mothers notice changes that might not seem obvious to other people."

I took a breath and opened my mouth, but she silenced me with a shake of her head. "I know you're not a talker, Brett. You are just as closed up as Eli. I also know that you have been carrying a lot of hurt inside your heart."

Her caring tone and the look of worry on her face had me turning mine away. I focused on Molly and Flynn throwing a Frisbee at each other while Dozer desperately tried to catch it mid-air.

"No," loving fingers forced my face back to hers. "Look at me, son. This is a small town; you already know that I know most of what's happening. I don't need details, but I need you to listen to me. Don't let bullheadedness keep you from what you're supposed to have."

She leveled me with a stare as the weight of her words settled. How could she possibly know that it wasn't stubbornness keeping me from Kenzie? I prided myself on not being a stupid man. Driving hundreds of miles to tell a woman that I loved her and could not breathe without her while knowing she didn't feel the same, was the very definition of stupid.

I didn't say that to Mrs. Jackson though. Instead, I nodded and went with "Yes, Ma'am." Her eyes warned she had more to say, but I think she took pity on me as she wordlessly dragged me to where everyone was huddled around the table.

She squeezed my arm before she moved to give her husband a kiss where he sat at his usual spot at the end of the table. Mr. Jackson pulled her close and stole another kiss before he allowed her to slip onto the chair next to him.

The relationship they shared reminded me so much of my own parents, maybe that was why I always felt like I was home when I was with them. After grabbing a beer from the cooler box, I moved to shake Mr. Jackson's hand. He squeezed it with a "Son, good to see you."

I greeted him and then dropped onto the empty chair at the other end of the table. My gaze bounced from one person to the next in greeting. As usual Logan and Harper were as close together as they could possibly get without being on top of each other. Chase was leaned back in his chair, his usual *I-don't-have-a-care-in-the-world-look* spread all over his demeanor. Opposite him, Eli was sporting a rare smile while he toyed with the label of his beer; I had no doubt he was watching his little girl.

The only one missing was Lizzy. She used to come to Friday BBQs all the time but, much like me, she just stopped. I had a suspicion it had something to do with Chase. It must be all sorts of awkward realizing you had feelings for someone who's supposed to be a friend.

I pressed deeper into the back of my chair and spread my legs wide. These were my people, and even though there would always be a hole the size of Texas in my chest, I still had them.

"Tell me, Brett," Mr. Jackson's voice broke through my thoughts. "When are you going to give those skills you have the attention they deserve?"

One year I'd made Mrs. Jackson a vase for her birthday and from then on Mr. Jackson had been on my case to open up my own studio. The thing was I was happy working at the shop.

"That's a good question, Pop." Logan joined in.

A grin lifted my lips, "If you're so eager for me to leave the shop, I could always come help out here."

Mr. Jackson smacked his hands together, "Now that's a splendid idea. Chris would only be too happy to have an extra set of hands." I wasn't fooled by the serious expression on the older man's face, my friend, however, was.

Just as Logan's brows started to pull together, the entire table burst out laughing. Even I joined in, and it felt great to just be in the moment with friends. A coughing fit stole Mr. Jackson's laughter which earned him a glare from his wife.

She shook her index finger at him, "Charles, you know you're not supposed to smoke." The look on Mr. Jackson's face was priceless. I had no doubt he was in for a long speech as soon as we left.

Mrs. Jackson gave him another pointed stare before turning her attention to Harper, her voice as sweet as honey. "So when can I get all dolled up and see my son get married, hmm?"

Logan chuckled and then side-eyed Harper, "I've been wondering the same thing, Momma." That earned him a smack to the chest from his beloved fiancée.

"I still don't have a dress. I barely have time these days and with there being no shop in Willow Creek…" She shrugged her shoulders.

"Aw, Sugar," Logan nudged her shoulder. "I don't care about the dress; it's what's underneath it that I want." The grin he gave her left no doubt in any of our minds what was on his.

Harper shook her head, and another bout of laughter erupted. At the other end of the table, Mr. Jackson's laugh morphed into another coughing fit. This time, though, his wife's backhand flew to his shoulder as she shook her head in disappointment.

We might have been laughing, but we also knew that Mrs. Jackson was worried about her husband's health. On more than one occasion I'd heard her say that she was terrified of the day she had to face the world without Charles Jackson by her side.

"I'm going to get started on the salad," Harper announced when the laughter died down, and she pushed to her feet and started walking toward the house only to stop next to me. "Wanna give me a hand?"

The way she demanded it, left no room for negotiation. "Uh, sure."

"What's the matter with you?"

I was about to take a swig from my beer when her hissing question stopped me mid-way. Curious, I scanned the kitchen to see if there was anyone else besides Harper and me in the kitchen. I saw no one, but still, I poked my chest and asked, "You talking to me?"

She planted her hands on her hips, "Yes you, dummy."

Did she want a list?

"You need to take a page out of Logan's book." She peeked through the window, and I followed her gaze. Everyone was still in deep conversation around the table. With her focus still on them, she murmured. "Do you think I would be here if he just gave up?"

Finally, I figured out what she was on about. "It's not the same, Harper."

She kept her gaze on the people outside a while longer before she turned her attention to me. "Fate has a funny way of meddling with our lives when we least expect it." Her smile looked wistful. "Did I ever tell you how I landed in Willow Creek?"

I shook my head after swallowing a few mouthfuls of beer.

"I opened a map and just picked the first place I saw. Now you tell me that fate didn't have a hand in that."

"Things are different with Kenzie, she has someone." Saying the words was equivalent to swallowing acid.

"You men can be so dumb sometimes, you know that? Brett, you need to get off your high horse and go get your woman."

I bit down hard on my teeth. "I don't see how this is any of your business."

Not even fazed by my pissiness, she curled her fingers around my wrist. "We're family, and that makes it my business. Did you even talk to her before she left?"

We did a bit more than talk. "I asked her to stay, and she still left. So yeah, I did talk to her."

She knitted her brows, and her eyes searched mine. "Well then, did you listen, I mean really listen to what she had to say?"

"I know you mean well, but I'm asking you to drop it." Done with the conversation, I spun on my heels and marched back outside.

KENZIE

Surprisingly I didn't feel as nervous as I thought I would when I opened my door. On the other side stood Dean decked out in another tailor-made suit that fit his frame perfectly. He flicked his wrist, pulled back his sleeve and smiled a nervous smile.

"I made reservations at that new French place you wanted to try out." His gaze swept over me. "Uh, shall I wait while you get changed?"

I was still wearing my jeans and off-the-shoulder blouse. Shaking my head, I opened the door further. "I thought we could stay in and order takeout?"

Dean looked at me as if I just spoke a foreign language and to an extent, maybe I had. I wish I could say I was one of those domestic goddesses that could whip up a meal a Michelin chef would be proud of. What I knew about cooking was limited to omelets and scrambled eggs.

If we weren't having dinner with potential clients at some fancy restaurant or with either of our parents, Dean used to cook for us. With a puzzled look on his face, he came inside, his eyes searching with every step.

I closed the door and headed straight for the kitchen, I grabbed a bottle of his favorite wine from the rack along with two glasses before I padded back to the living room. Dean had shrugged out of his jacket and loosened his tie slightly. With his hands on his hips, he paced in front of the fireplace.

"Wine?"

He turned to face me, regarded the wine I held up and shook his head. "Kenzie, what's going on? You've been acting strange for a while."

After setting the glasses and unopened wine on the coffee table, I perched on the edge of my couch. He paced some more and even from where I was sitting I could feel his frustration.

With a sigh, he lowered his frame to the seat opposite me. Legs spread wide, arms folded, he waited.

I took a breath and began, "I have to tell you something and for you to at least understand some of it, I need to start at the beginning—" He listened as I told him about my relationship with Brett, how he'd given up his freedom for me and how my parents had kept us apart.

"It's a sad story," he remarked. "But I don't understand what it has to do with us."

"You will in a minute," Eyeing the wine, I cursed the fact that it was still sealed. "While I waited for my car to get fixed, I ran into Brett." I paused and waited for the weight of my words to settle. When realization dawned on his face, I continued, "I don't know how to say this, so I'm just going to say it."

Dean turned his head to the fireplace, and I knew that he knew what I was about to confess. "We kissed."

Frowning, his gaze snapped to mine, "Just a kiss?"

Oh, it was so much more than that. He breathed life into my lungs with that kiss. "Yes." I wrung my hands together in my lap as I tried to find the words that kept eluding me.

"After all these years, you're still in love with him?"

I looked up from my fidgeting hands, "I am," the confession came without hesitation. "Dean, you're a good man—"

"Just not the right one, apparently."

"Not for me, no." I pushed to my feet and took another breath. "I could—*should*—tell you how sorry I am, but I can't. It's hard to regret something that felt so right." Once I started, I couldn't stop the words from coming. "And to be honest, I don't think you and I really love each other."

Dean jumped up, "I asked you to move in with me, how can you say I don't love you?"

"You only asked because our mothers pushed you into doing it."

He opened his mouth and then shut it abruptly, pulling his lips into a thin line. Tentatively, I approached him and placed my hand on his arm. "I'm not saying that we don't care for each other, I think it's more a case of us growing comfortable with one another, you know?"

He side-eyed me, his mouth still stretched thin. "Are you going to him?" he asked.

I shook my head, "I don't know, I have a lot of things to figure out."

"Well, good luck with that." Dean pulled away from me and grabbed his jacket off the armrest of the couch. Thrusting his arms into the expensive fabric, he glared at me. "If you think I'm going to stand here and congratulate you on ripping the ground right from under me, you're wrong."

He stomped to the door, yanked it open and then paused to give me another angry stare. "Amongst those things you need to figure out, make sure you put love and loyalty right at the top. Clearly, you are clueless." The slamming door signaled not only his departure from my apartment but my life too.

Not caring that it was in the middle of the night, I raced up Zoe's steps and banged on her door. I waited and waited, but no one came. Walking backward, I looked up and scanned the row of windows.

Soft yellow wisps spilled from her bedroom, I marched back to the front door and banged louder this time. I had to pound my fists against the wood another few times before the door flew open revealing a half-naked man—a sweaty, half-naked man.

"Uh," I tried to peek around his broad shoulders, but his bulk filled the frame. "Is Zoe home?"

Half-naked Guy's lips lifted into a salacious grin. "She's a little tied up at the moment."

This is what I get for showing up without calling first. "Who's at the door, Andy?" Zoe's voice carried through the house.

Andy aimed a questioning look in my direction. Instead of answering him, I did something that I had never done before. I pushed past him and bounded up the stairs.

Big mistake. Trust me, it didn't matter if two people were as close as sisters, no one needed to see their friend's goodies on display like that. "I'm sorry," I yelped as I quickly turned around and covered my eyes.

"Kenzie? What the hell are you doing here?"

"Clearly interrupting something, but I kinda need to talk to you." Leaning my forehead against the wall in front of me, I breathed out "I broke up with Dean."

"You what?" I heard her tug and pull on the restraints around her arms and legs. "Ugh, Andy!"

A second later Andy came sauntering in, "She joining us?"

"No, you big oaf." More tugging and pulling. "Untie me," Zoe demanded.

"But we just—"

"Andy!"

There was something very wrong with me because all I wanted to do was giggle like a little schoolgirl. "I'll just wait downstairs." I raced back down the stairs. So fast, that I stumbled on the bottom few. My arm flew to the side as I steadied myself against the wall.

Maybe it was shock or just the emotional toll of the day, but I burst out laughing and couldn't stop. I moved to the far end of Zoe's living room where she kept her easel and paint supplies. After a few—more like a lot of—steadying breaths I finally regained my composure. Turning my attention to the window, with nothing but darkness behind it, I felt panic creep up my spine.

What the hell am I going to do?

My hands flew to my face and this time thick, hot tears spilled from my eyes. Yeah, I was a mess alright.

"Hey," Zoe appeared in front of me and pulled me in for a hug which felt a bit awkward considering how short she was. But awkward or not, it felt good to be comforted, and that just made me cry even harder. "Sweetie, you're scaring me," my friend whispered.

I pulled away from her slightly and wiped my eyes with the heels of my palms. "I'm sorry." My gaze traveled to the staircase, and I wondered if Andy was up there waiting for Zoe.

As if she heard my silent question, she answered, "He went home."

Scrunching up my nose, I looked at her, "I ruined your night, didn't I? I'm a horrible friend."

"Pfft," she nonchalantly sliced her arm through the air, and then her brown eyes turned serious, "You needed me, that's more important."

Like a hormonal mess, I wanted to bawl my eyes out again, but by some miracle, I managed to keep the tears at bay. I followed Zoe to her little kitchen where she made us hot chocolate—aka her cure for everything.

"Okay, Kenz, tell me what happened," she urged after we seated ourselves at her dinette.

With both my hands wrapped around the mug, I cradled it to my chest and told Zoe about how my dad had arranged for mine and Brett's letters to be intercepted. I also confessed that the methylphenidate was mine and not his. Of course, that news didn't surprise her nor did it bother her.

"—so after we figured out what really happened," I paused to take a sip of my warm chocolate drink. "He kissed me." Nibbling on my lip, I waited for her reaction.

Zoe's face remained void of emotion for a few seconds before her lips started to twitch and a wide smile broke free. "I told you to get closure, not jump his bones."

My own smile spread across my face while I shook my head. "There was no jumping on any bones."

My friend's cheerful laughter filled the space around us. She flicked her blonde locks over her shoulder and pushed her shoulders back, "Well that's bloody unfortunate." She laughed again, but this time my smile faltered as I remembered what happened right after that amazing kiss. Zoe stood and slipped onto the chair next to me. Touching my shoulder, she said, "It was just a joke, Sweetie."

I patted her hand, "It's not that." Staring into my mug, I relived my last few moments with Brett. "He is just so infuriating!" I voiced my thoughts. "A stubborn, thick-headed man who refuses to see reason."

"And yet, you love him," Zoe stated. I didn't have to see it to know she was smiling at me.

"So much," I conceded when I turned my gaze to her.

My friend pushed to her feet and planted her fists on her rounded hips, "Then go to him." She snatched the mug from me and placed it on the table before she grabbed both my hands. "Take a leap of faith, Kenzie!"

BRETT

INSTEAD OF HEADING INSIDE MY CABIN WHEN I ARRIVED HOME, I went to my workshop. It was the only place that filled me with a sense of pride. In there I had the freedom to be creative and artistic. I had often wondered what my parents would have made of it. I imagined them smiling with delight at every piece I created.

Normally I'd fire up my machinery; I wasn't in the mood to craft something big. My little sanctuary was by no means one of those extravagant studios you'd find in the city, I didn't have fancy furnaces or industrial crucibles but what I had got the job done. Besides, blowing glass was more of a hobby than a business.

Sparking the blowtorch to life, I pulled a stool closer and grabbed two thick tubes of glass. I had no idea what I was going to make, I just needed to lose myself in the process. Except for running, few things gave me the sense of calmness I always got from molding molten glass into something beautiful and delicate.

The blue and orange started its hypnotizing dance as I pushed the ends of both tubes into the flame. Constantly rotating them my mind drifted to what Harper had told me. The less I wanted to believe it actually existed, the more fate proved me wrong.

I kept rotating the glass, only touching them to each other here and there. When I had a big enough ball on one tube, I set the other down and used my tweezers to start manipulating the warm glass.

Again, my mind drifted back to Logan and Harper. Their relationship wasn't received with open arms. She'd arrived in town with nothing but secrets, and his reputation left a lot to be desired. Still, they made it work.

As I continued to shape the glass, alternating between using my tweezers and scoring knife, I forced myself to think—*really think*—about the last time I saw Kenzie. Over the last couple of days, I must've replayed that kiss endless times, but I always forced my brain to another place instead of reliving that conversation.

I tilted my hand up and went to pull the glass in another direction. *'I need to sort things out with Dean'*, her sweet voice rang in my ears. I pulled my brows together. *'When I'm with you I don't want anything between us, especially not guilt.'*

My hands stilled, and I removed the piece of glass from the fire. "Shit!" The curse rumbled from the very pit of my stomach. Harper was absolutely right; I was as stupid as they came. How the hell did I misread the situation so horribly?

Maybe it was because I was more concerned with my ego taking a bashing than I was with actual words spilling from her lips. My girl hadn't thrown me away. She needed breathing room to figure her own stuff out and being the pigheaded asshole that I was, I'd chased her away.

I glanced down at the tiny sculpture in progress and grinned. "Yeah, yeah, I know you exist. No need to show off." A glint of light bounced off the butterfly in the making, and I swore it was fate winking at me.

"Should I be afraid?" Logan asked when he opened the door the following morning. It was just after five, and although I knew it was in bad taste to hammer someone's door down that early, I couldn't help it.

I took in his still half-asleep appearance and grimaced, "Sorry. Did I wake Flynn too?"

"Nah, I peeked into his room on my way to the door. My little man is lost in dreamland." He looked me over and then asked, "What's up?"

"So, your soon-to-be wife shed some light on things, and I need to head out of town for a bit. That alright?" He might've been my friend, but he was still my employer as well.

A slow smile spread across his lips, and he propped his shoulder against the doorframe. "You gonna go get your girl?"

"Damn right, I am."

"About friggin time."

I let out a hearty laugh. "Yeah, I know." I clapped him on the shoulder and after a quick, "Thanks, man," I rushed back to my truck.

Sweetheart, I'm coming and I ain't leaving without you.

KENZIE

"IT'S OKAY TO BE NERVOUS."

I took in the strewn about clothes and open suitcases on my bed. "What if I'm making a mistake?"

Zoe pushed a few items aside and perched herself on the edge of the bed, "Look, Kenz, I can't tell you that, but I can tell you that not doing this will be the biggest mistake you'll ever make. You owe it to yourself to go find out what could possibly be."

I'd made the decision in Zoe's kitchen that I was going to Willow Creek and I wasn't leaving until that thick-headed man heard everything I had to say. Even if he didn't want to listen to it, I was going to tell him exactly how much I loved him.

A huge part of me was scared beyond belief. All my life I'd taken the easy way out of everything. I'd blindly accepted that I wasn't in charge of my future. As much as knowing the truth was liberating it was also terrifying.

For the first time in my life, I had no direction. I didn't know what the future held. The only thing I knew for certain was that I wasn't going to sit around and let other people plan my future. If I crashed and burned, it was going to be on my terms.

I straightened my spine and squared my shoulders, "You're absolutely right." With a smile on my face and hope in my heart, I started packing my new clothes. Zoe and I had worked in a quick trip to the shops early that morning. It was kind of refreshing to swap my stifling business suits for more casual clothes.

Zoe held up a pair of denim cut-offs with white lace worked into the sides. She had been adamant that I buy it. "You're so wearing this!" She jumped up and started rummaging through the clothes still on the bed. "Oooh and this too." In her hands was a skimpy white top with a plunging neckline; another one of her selections.

I raised an eyebrow, "Do you want me to seduce him or lay my heart bare?"

Zoe shrugged, "This does both."

A welcomed laugh bubbled to the surface as I snatched the items from her and stuffed them into the suitcase.

"Ah, boo," she whined.

I walked over to her and playfully poked her shoulder, "In that shirt, my chest is going to have his undivided attention, not the words coming out of my mouth." Sadness washed over me, and I immediately wrapped my arms around Zoe, "I'm going to miss your face."

"Aw, Kenz, I'm going to miss the crap out of you, but—" she pushed me away slightly, and I didn't even have to hear the words, I saw it shining in her eyes. "—I'm so damn proud of you." She swatted my butt and ordered, "Now, come on. No time for tears, we have to get you all packed up so you can go get your man!"

This time when I approached the enormous white door, I wasn't as nervous as I'd been the day before. I drew strength from the fact that I was doing something for me. With a deep breath, I wrapped my fingers around the knocker. Moments after two sharp knocks sounded, Selma, who was wearing a huge smile, ushered me inside.

I followed her through the house to where my parents were sitting on the patio. My mother's nose was buried in a magazine while my father browsed through the newspaper. He was the first one to spot me, and although I had nothing to feel ashamed of, the look of disapproval he gave me still hurt.

Placing the newspaper on the glass table in front of him, he leaned back and crossed one leg over the other. "I assume you're here to apologize for your appalling behavior yesterday."

At my father's harsh words, my mother looked up, her eyes widening when she saw me. "Dean's mother called this morning."

"Of course she did," I took a fortifying breath through my nose and addressed my father, "No, Daddy, I'm not."

My father lifted his chin and turned his attention to the Olympic sized swimming pool that no one ever used. "Well, then we have nothing to talk about." My mother's gaze bounced between my dad and me, and I could have sworn I saw conflict spread all over her face.

"That's okay, you don't have to talk. Just listen." I wiped my palms on my jeans and drew from the pride I saw in my friend's eyes. "I didn't want to leave without saying goodbye."

My dad's eyes snapped to mine, I didn't even recognize the man glaring daggers at me. "You might want to rethink that before you end up on top of the midden along with the rest of the trash."

"One man's trash is another man's treasure." I stole a glance at my mother who was being strangely quiet in the matter. "You might not understand this, Daddy, but I love Brett."

His face started to turn red, "How can you love a man who you haven't seen in over a decade? You're throwing away everything you've worked for. For what?"

Shaking my head, I pushed my sadness away. "Why can't you just be happy for me?"

Rushing to his feet, my father seethed, "Be happy for you? You're throwing everything we've ever done for you back in our faces."

"You're so oblivious," I said softly. "I never wanted the fancy schools or expensive gifts. The only thing I ever wanted, the only thing I still want, is for you to be proud of who *I* am. Not the person you want me to be." I sucked in a breath and padded to my father.

Tentatively I placed my hand on his arm and pleaded, "It doesn't matter how much we fight or for how long, I'll always love you and mom. I just really need you to tell me it's okay for me to chase my own dreams for a change."

My father's eyes met mine; they reminded me so much of my own. "I can't tell you that." In a matter of seconds, the ground got ripped from beneath me. My stomach rolled, and my heart hurt as my dad pulled his arm away from me.

"If you leave here today and go after that man, you can consider yourself without parents."

I gasped, and my mother's hands flew to her mouth. Still, she didn't utter a word. I wanted to stomp over and shake her because Diana Michaels always had something to say. "But—" my father went on as if he didn't just turn my world on its axis. "—if you stay and admit the error of your ways, I'm sure I can smooth things over with Dean and his parents."

Tears spilled from my eyes, and I made no attempt to wipe them away. I looked at my mom, hoping to silently plead with her not to let my father take these drastic measures, but the moment our gazes locked she looked away.

Realizing that nothing I could ever say would change their minds, I took a step backward. I pulled a piece of paper from my back pocket and placed it on the table. "The address on top is for the guesthouse I stayed at in Willow Creek," my voice wobbled, and I had to clear my throat before I could speak again. "The one at the bottom is Brett's. If you change your mind, I should be at either of those places." I sucked in a breath and lifted my chin. "I'm really hoping it's the bottom one, though."

I spun on my heels and started for the door only to be halted by my mother's, "Kenzie!" Slowly, I turned to face her; tears were streaming down her face. Out of the corner of my eye, I noticed my father approaching her. He placed his hand on her shoulder and then turned his scowl to me, "Let her go, Diana."

Determined to walk out of my parents' home with my head held high, I resisted the urge to run as fast as my feet would carry me. By the time I drove past the city limits, I knew without a doubt that I wasn't making a mistake.

BRETT

I PULLED MY PHONE OUT OF MY POCKET AND OPENED THE *NOTES* APPLICATION. After a quick glance at the number on the building, I rechecked my phone . I was in the right place alright. Well, at least I was at the address I'd gotten from Kenzie's job card. I could have easily called her to make sure, but I needed the element of surprise on my side. I was afraid that if I gave her too much of a heads-up, she'd find an excuse not to see me. After my behavior, I deserved nothing less.

Yanking on the rearview mirror, I adjusted it so I could see my reflection before I dragged my fingers through my hair. I smoothed my palm over the strands a few times before doing the same to my beard. I wasn't sure if I was trying to look my best or if I was just stalling.

Maybe it was both.

With my heart pounding against my ribs, I unfolded myself from my truck and walked toward the impressive building. I couldn't tell you how many floors it had, I just knew that Kenzie's apartment was supposedly on the fifth floor—that was *all* I needed to know about the place.

As soon as I entered, I wondered if I was walking into an apartment complex or a five-star hotel. I was confident I looked more than a little out of place in my faded jeans and a blue flannel shirt.

Not even giving the elevators a glance, I headed straight for the stairs, taking them two at a time. The long hallway that greeted me after the fourth flight of stairs seemed endless. I sucked in a few steadying breaths and willed myself to calm the hell down. Being as nervous as I was wasn't normal for me, but that was only a testament to how important this day was.

Nothing but determination pushed me forward. I scanned each door as I passed it until I found the one I was looking for. My past, my present, and, hopefully, my future was behind that door.

Lifting my hand, I tapped my knuckles against the wood twice. I drew in a breath and held it when I heard shuffling inside. It felt like forever before the door swung open, when it did, though, a deep frown pulled my brows together.

"Zoe?" I didn't know how she did it, but Zoe Carlisle hadn't aged a bit since our college days. She flicked her blonde locks and propped her shoulder against the doorjamb. After giving me an assessing once over, she crossed her arms.

"Well, well, well," she chirped. "If it isn't Brett Carter in the flesh."

From the doorway, I scanned as much of the apartment as I could. What I saw had my heart dropping to my feet. Boxes. Not just any boxes, those were the kind of boxes you used when you were moving. "I…uh…" As I tried to speak past the cotton wool in my throat, I hoped that I had the wrong address. "I'm looking for Kenzie, she here?"

Zoe narrowed her eyes and pursed her lips. "About damn time, buuuut—" she singsonged. "—you're too late, my friend."

In frustration, I raked my fingers through my hair and turned to face the door on the opposite side. I blew out a breath and faced Zoe again. "Where can I find her?"

Her shoulders rose and fell, "I can't be sure; she mentioned something about going to see the man of her dreams and begging him to let her have his babies."

Like hell she is. The only man whose babies she's gonna have is mine. Maybe those kinds of thoughts made me sound like a Neanderthal, but I didn't care. Just the mere thought of another man touching her, had me clenching my fist and gritting my teeth.

Zoe's soft laugh reached my ears before her, "Whoa there, don't go turning green on me." She pushed off the frame and patted my chest in a way that said *'there, there.'* "I really can't tell you where she is. Not because I don't know but I promised her I wouldn't. However—" she held up her finger. "—between you and me, she wouldn't go anywhere without saying goodbye to her parents."

Mr. and Mrs. Michaels. Speaking with them had been on my agenda too, I'd just hoped that I would get to talk to Kenzie first. With a quick, "thanks", I retraced my steps back to the truck. After typing the address in my maps application, I turned the key, and the truck rumbled to life.

I practiced what to say over and over while navigating through the traffic. Cities weren't for me anymore, I'd felt caged in the moment the tall buildings had come into view. But if this was where Kenzie's life was, I'd make the change for her.

When I'd left Willow Creek, I had been determined that I would bring her back with me. I hadn't reckoned in the fact that she had family and friends, not to mention her job. It would be selfish to ask her to give it all up.

No, I wouldn't do that. I needed her more than I needed open spaces and quiet. The voice on the application told me I had arrived at my destination. I stared at the three-story building and mused to myself that the only good thing that ever came out of it was Kenzie.

Slowing to a roll, I followed the rounded driveway that led to the house. To my right and left were expertly trimmed shrubs in various sizes and colors. Even with the window closed, the sound of running water filled my ears. I looked around and counted eight strategically placed fountains.

There was no doubt that it was as beautiful as it was impressive, but I wondered how often they actually came outside and just enjoyed the view. To my right I spotted a tree with thick, reaching branches; it would be the perfect spot to build a swing or a tree house.

I knew that Kenzie didn't have those things growing up; it didn't fit into her parents' plan for her life. Turning off the ignition, I stared at the big, white doors and vowed that if she'd let me, I'd give her all those things and more.

The walk from my truck to the front of the house felt equivalent to walking the plank. With every step I took, I searched and searched but didn't see a red Mazda anywhere. Well, I was here now. I pulled the golden knocker and dropped it twice.

On the other side of the open door stood a short, plump woman with gray-streaked black hair. She looked older, but I could have sworn it was the same woman who worked here when Kenzie and I had dated.

"I would like to speak to Mr. and Mrs. Michaels, please." I inhaled deeply. "It's important."

She made a face, and I was sure she was about to tell me to get off the property, but then she motioned for me to come inside. Once she closed the door, she spoke in a hushed tone, "Follow me."

Silently, I trailed behind her as she led me down a hallway into a room I assumed was Mr. Michaels' office. "Wait here," she ordered before she turned to leave.

"Thank you," I muttered at her retreating back.

There was no way I would be able to sit still. I moved to the bookcase and inspected the items on it. Running a finger across their spines, I took note of some of Mr. Michaels' reading materials: *The Art of War, Memoirs of an Infantry Officer, The War Poems, The Old Huntsman.*

A myriad of business awards adorned the shelves along with the books and art pieces, but it was a photo of a young Kenzie that caught my eye. She had to be about seven or eight in it. Usually, kids that age would be grinning at the camera, showing off their teeth—or gums. Not in this picture though. With her back ramrod straight, Kenzie sat behind a desk with an expression so serious it made my heart hurt.

"Ah, that's a wonderful photo."

The suddenness of her father's voice startled me. I returned the photo to its spot and walked over to the man who'd just entered the room. With my hand held out, I greeted him, "Mr. Michaels. My name is—"

"I know who you are," he looked at my outstretched hand but made no move to grip it. "What do you want?"

Just as I dropped my hand, Mrs. Michaels entered. I might've been wrong, but the woman looked like she'd been crying. Without acknowledging me, she turned to her husband. "Shall I ask Selma to bring in refreshments?"

Mr. Michaels' harsh, "No," bounced off the walls. If he thought that he was going to intimidate me, he was wrong. "What. Do. You. Want?" He punctuated each word as though he was speaking to a child.

I widened my stance and clasped my hands in front of me. "My momma raised me right, Sir. She'd want me to come here and ask for your blessing." He opened his mouth to say something, I interjected, "But, I can't do that. You see," I continued. "If I asked, you wouldn't let me love your daughter. I don't fit into your plan, and that's okay."

The man's jaw muscle ticked in irritation, I wasn't fazed. "Mr. Michaels, your daughter doesn't just fit into *my* plans; there is no plan without her. I love your daughter, and there isn't a thing I wouldn't do for her." I leveled him with a stare. "*You* should know that."

Mrs. Michaels had the decency to look ashamed but her husband just puffed up his chest. "I don't need your permission to love your daughter; I just need her to allow me to do it. And for Kenzie's sake, I hope you can accept that."

He tilted his nose skyward and narrowed his eyes. I saw the judgment before I heard it. "You'll never be good enough for her."

"Oh, you're right," I agreed. "But I will spend every minute of every day doing my damnedest to be the man she deserves."

Mr. Michaels shook an accusatory finger at me. "It's because you've filled her head with this garbage that she has thrown away everything she's worked for. What kind of life will she have in that town of yours?"

He was still rambling, but my ears stopped listening. Kenzie was on her way to Willow Creek. My feet started to move before my brain could even issue the command. "Mr. and Mrs. Michaels, thank you for your time." I didn't wait to hear what they said and frankly I didn't care.

I needed to catch up to my girl.

BRETT

DRIVING AS FAST AS THE SPEED LIMIT ALLOWED FOR WASN'T FAST ENOUGH. For what felt like the hundredth time in the past two-and-a-half hours, I pulled up Kenzie's number and poked the green button. As sweet as it was to hear her voice tell me I should try again later, I would have much rather preferred to hear it from her lips.

Anxious, excited, worried. I felt them all in freaking spades. And the fact that her phone kept going to voicemail wasn't helping matters much, either. I gripped the steering wheel tighter and accelerated a bit. My mind was still reeling from the fact that my woman was on her way to Willow Creek.

Now, her daddy hadn't used those exact words, but it didn't take a genius to figure out. I thought of the kind of life she'd had growing up, and I made a silent promise that our kids wouldn't know that kind of life. Yeah, I was getting ahead of myself, but I hadn't lied to Mr. Michaels. I didn't want a future without Kenzie in it, and I was going to do everything I could to make that happen.

Out in the distance, I saw something hobble into the road. I blinked a couple of times, thinking my tired mind must be playing tricks on me. It wasn't. I swerved and brought my truck to an abrupt halt. After jumping out, I checked for traffic in both directions before I hurried to where the ball of fur had collapsed.

I narrowed my eyes and scanned the immediate area; there was nothing but dry land for miles. Carefully, I dropped to my haunches, "Where did ya come from, little buddy?" The dog lifted its head and let out a little moan before making a feeble attempt to lick me.

There was no way I could leave the animal there. I rushed back to the truck and gripped my jacket from the backseat before hurrying back to the dog. With caution, I stroked its head, "I'm gonna help you, okay? No biting."

A little whimper sounded from the ball of fur when I threw my jacket over it and gathered it into my arms. After I gently placed it on the passenger side floor, searched for something to drink for the poor animal. All I found was a bunch of candy bar wrappers and empty soda cans.

I had been in such a hurry to get back on the road that I hadn't even thought about food or drink; the growl in my stomach reminding me of that. I climbed behind the wheel and eased back onto the road. After a quick call to Chase, I tried Kenzie's number again. No luck.

As my impatience reached its height, I stomped my foot down on the gas, and the rest of my two-hour drive was done in one-and-a-half. I couldn't remember ever feeling that happy as I drove past the *Welcome to Willow* Creek sign.

I threw my truck into park in front of the clinic and rushed around to the passenger side. I yanked open the door, and as the ball of fur lifted its head, its lids parted to reveal the most striking blue eyes. The color reminded me of Kenzie's favorite butterfly, the Holly blue.

Gathering the animal in my arms, I rushed inside. Chase was already waiting for us, and I followed him to the exam room. The sterile smell of disinfectant hit my nose the moment I entered. I placed the dog on the stainless steel table but kept a comforting hand on it while Chase snapped on disposable latex gloves.

"So you found this little guy or girl in the middle of the road?"

My gaze dropped to the dog, "Yeah, I don't know if someone just left it or what, but it was limping before it slumped to the ground."

Chase bent so he was eye-level with the animal, he pinched the skin between the shoulders together and made a humming sound. Placing his fingers behind its jaw, he pressed a couple of times before moving to its abdomen.

It felt like the examination took forever and as desperately as I wanted to find Kenzie, I needed to know that the dog was okay.

"Okay," Chase began while he pulled the gloves off and threw them in a bin under the table. "She is definitely dehydrated and malnourished. It's a good thing you found her when you did. I'll need to take an x-ray of her leg, but I don't think it's broken." He scratched her behind the ear. "I'll get her started on an IV, and we'll go from there."

I nodded while dragging my palm over the back of my neck. "What's going to happen to her when she's all healed up?"

Chase shrugged, "She'll end up in the den." The den was where they kept all the animals that needed forever homes.

For some reason that didn't sit well with me. "Can I keep her?"

"I see no reason why not."

Sucking in a breath and blowing it out through my nose, I answered, "Great." I pulled my phone out of my pocket to check the time then to Chase I asked, "Can I fill in all the paperwork tomorrow? I really need to go. Kenzie is…somewhere in town, and I need to find her."

His lips lifted into a smile and a "Sure, man," followed. I gave the dog a quick scratch and promised to check on her in the morning. After a smack against Chase's shoulder, I made a dash for my truck.

By my calculations, Kenzie could've been at one of three places: The Guesthouse, the Diner, or my cabin. I decided to skip ahead to the last one. Normally when I drove to my cabin, I enjoyed a nice slow drive to better appreciate the scenery. Not this time though. I came barreling down the road with a cloud of dust licking at my heels.

I noticed the back of Kenzie's Mazda peeking out next to the cabin, and I almost stopped short. Even though I had a fairly good idea that she was headed to Willow Creek, I still had to blink a couple of times to be sure that I wasn't dreaming.

As I drew closer, my lips stretched into a wide smile. There was no doubt that the views surrounding my cabin were magnificent but none of it compared to the sight of Kenzie sitting on her car's hood; legs stretched out, and her head tilted to the sky.

Chapter 31

KENZIE

I HEARD THE RUMBLE OF BRETT'S TRUCK LONG BEFORE I ACTUALLY SAW HIM. It had taken superhuman strength to stay seated and not jump off and sprint toward him. Most of the drive down to Willow Creek had been done with tears rolling down my cheeks. My parents might have had their faults—like everyone else—but I still loved them. The way I left things with them wasn't ideal, and I hoped that there would come a time real soon where they understood why I did what I did.

It took me almost my entire adult life to realize it was okay to do something just for me. My dreams were important too. Although right at that second the only dream I was certain of was barreling toward me, leaving a dust cloud in his wake.

The truck rolled to a stop and Brett, and I made eye contact through his windshield. Again, I had to force myself to stay put when all I wanted to do was launch myself at him. His door swung open, the hinges moaning out a squeak, and then he emerged looking dangerously sexy. Hair mussed from probably dragging his fingers through it a few times too many. Even though his tiredness was reflected in them, his eyes glistened with expectation.

I nibbled on my lip as he approached me, the muscles beneath his jeans bulging with every step and the flannel stretching over his chest just begged to be ripped off. His gaze slid over my body with unmasked appreciation giving me tingles all over. He came to a stop in front of the car and placed his hands over my ankles. Those lips of his curved into a sinful half-smile before he yanked me to him.

The laughter that erupted from me couldn't be helped one bit. Brett slid his fingers into my hair, with his hand cradling my head he pulled my face to his. With our noses almost touching, he murmured, "You're awfully far from home." The warmth of his breath breezed over my lips.

My fingers curled around his twitching biceps, "Am I?" I tilted my chin in the direction of the cabin. "I thought that was home."

His mouth came down over mine so fast, it stole my breath. It took me a second, but when I regained my composure, I kissed him right back. My tongue matching his, stroke for delicious stroke. I wanted to climb into that kiss and live there, possibly forever.

Brett's fingers dug into my skull as he held my mouth to his and continued to consume me so completely. By wrapping my legs around his waist I was able to get even closer to him, but it still wasn't close enough.

A low guttural moan rumbled from his chest and much to my dismay he broke our kiss and pulled away slightly. Using his thumb, he smoothed the frown; I never knew I had, from my forehead before cupping my cheeks.

"Sweetheart, I want you—" he looked down and smiled. "—you *know* I do. Talk first, hmm?"

I ran my tongue over my lip, I could still taste him there. "Talk?"

Brett touched his lips to mine in a way-too-quick kiss before he helped me down. He tucked me under his arm, and we started on the short walk to the cabin. The only problem was now that I was free to be with him, I wanted to *be* with him. And his thigh brushing against mine along with the warmth radiating off his body was doing nothing to calm the white-hot need that pulsed through my body.

Have you ever experienced such an intense need to do something that you just couldn't function properly until you got that damn monkey off your back? Well, if you multiplied that feeling by a hundred, you might understand why when Brett shut the door behind us, I pounced.

He barely had time to turn around when I flung myself at him. Wrapping my arms and legs around him and pressing my mouth wherever I found an open spot. His mouth opened, but I stole the protest from his tongue.

The groan that broke free vibrated through my body and I smiled a victorious smile when Brett gave into the kiss. I tasted his hunger, I felt his need and mine matched it. His hands slid up my thighs, his fingers dug into my butt. Before I had time to process that we were moving, my back made contact with his couch. Brett came down over me, and I swear the look in his eyes almost had me coming apart right there. His gaze was predatory, hungry, and, loving—so much love shone in his hazel eyes.

Our mouths fused together again and our clothed bodies moved to a frantic rhythm. Brett dragged his hands up my torso, taking my blouse along for the sensuous ride. With deft precision, it was tugged over my head and dropped to the floor.

His lips teased my collarbone before moving between my breasts, I arched my back in an effort to get closer to him. I needed so much more. I heard him inhale deeply before he whispered against my skin, "After all these years, you still use the same perfume."

"It used to be your favorite smell."

His mouth moved to my ribs trailing kisses along them that were achingly soft. "*You* are my favorite everything."

And just like that, he shifted his weight, so he was lying beside me with one leg draped over me. "Bre—" He silenced me by pressing his finger against my mouth.

"There are some things that you need to hear." His Adam's apple bobbed while the seriousness in his eyes pulled me from my lust-bubble. I nodded meekly, his gaze swept over my face and focused on the strand of hair he was brushing away. "I have been angry for a long time, Sweetheart." He shook his head. "I can't even remember the last time I experienced any other emotion."

I opened my mouth again, and he ran the pad of his thumb over my cheek. "Shh, just listen for a sec." His thumb brushed over my lips. "The thing is, my heart hurt for so long, I stopped listening to it. I couldn't see reason even when it was smacking me in the face. I'm sorry I didn't listen to you." Brett dropped a whisper of a kiss to my forehead. "I'm a thickheaded idiot."

Oh, you're thick alright. I pressed my lips together to keep the adolescent words from slipping out and ruining the moment. "But this thickheaded idiot," he went on, oblivious to my thoughts. "Wants to be yours. Kenzie, I love you so much, it's scary. It consumes me morning, afternoon, and, night. I know your daddy doesn't want—"

I pushed onto my elbow and took his face in my hands. "It's not about what they want, it's about us. Just us."

He slanted his mouth over mine again in a kiss so breathtakingly sweet and tender; it brought a fresh batch of tears to my eyes. "I saw them today," he breathed against my mouth.

"Who?" I asked absently. With my eyes closed, I drank in his kiss and got lost in his touch.

"Your parents." My lids snapped open, and I shot into a seated position.

"What? How? When?" I fired off the questions wondering why he went to my parents and never came to me.

The smile on his lips said he knew exactly what I was thinking. Brett pushed to his feet and left the room. He friggin left, leaving me to gape after him. A minute later he came sauntering back into the living room with two beers in one hand and a patchwork blanket hanging over his arm.

He set the drinks on the coffee table and then draped the blanket over my shoulders. "Brett! When did you see my parents?" Another thought popped into my head. What if my parents understood why I left and they came to Willow Creek to make amends?

His grin widened as he continued to cover me up. "In a minute, Sweetheart." He pulled the ends of the fabric together. "You're distracting." When I did nothing but shoot daggers at him, he laughed. "Okay, okay. My plan to go to the city and make some declaration of love kinda fell through when I arrived at your apartment and ran into Zoe."

"You went to the city to see me?" Like a moron, I repeated his words.

Brett didn't seem to mind though; he tucked a strand of hair behind my ear, "No Sweetheart. Not to see you but to make you mine." I turned to mush right there on his couch. *Silly man*. If he only knew, I'd been his all along.

"Anyway," he went on. "Zoe sent me to your parents," he winked. "You weren't there either, so I took the opportunity to tell your father what my intentions were."

"What did he say?"

His smile faltered slightly, but he recovered quickly. "Doesn't matter. You're here now, and I hope this means you're staying."

I threw the blanket off of my shoulders and crawled into his lap. There were no words that would ever do what I felt for this man, justice. The only thing I could do was touch my mouth to his and hope that my kiss would convey what I was unable to voice.

Chapter 32

BRETT

WITH HER MOUTH OVER MINE, KENZIE BREATHED LIFE INTO MY LUNGS. Every bold stroke of her tongue filled my heart with love and had want spreading through my entire body. With my fingers splayed on the bare skin of her back, I marveled in the feel of its softness.

I moved my mouth to her ear before I planted a trail of kisses down the slender column of her throat. She threw her head back, and gave me better access. I took my time kissing and nibbling on her skin when all I wanted to do was yank her beneath me and claim her properly.

The little needy whimpers sounding from her wasn't helping my resolve much. I hooked my fingers beneath her bra straps and slid them down as far as they would go. My lips close behind. As I inhaled her, my senses were assaulted in the best way possible. She was breathtakingly intoxicating.

As much as I liked Kenzie's hips rocking into my lap, I wanted her sprawled out on my bed where I could love on every inch of her body. I gathered her close to me and walked us to the bedroom without removing my lips from her skin. We were chest-to-chest, the erratic rhythm of her heart matching my own.

I lowered her to the bed, her eyes a deep shade of navy and her whole body beckoning me. The bed dipped under my weight as I first placed one knee and then the other on either side of her. Kenzie's hand disappeared between her breasts, and a second later the silk and lace that covered them fell away.

My fingers twitched, and I pulled my lip between my teeth to stop myself from ravishing her like the ravenous beast I was. "Oh, Sweetheart, I'm going to devour you."

She sucked her bottom lip into her mouth, and I descended, taking her mouth in a rough kiss. Kenzie's hands slid over my arms and her back arched, her body begging to be touched, to be loved.

Who was I to deny the request?

I ached, painfully so. Still, I took my time as I thoroughly loved on the newly exposed skin. Beneath me, my girl had turned into a moaning, writhing bundle of bones. Man, it was the most beautiful sight. Torturously slow, I unsnapped the button of her jeans and pulled them down her legs.

I threw the fabric over my shoulder and caught a glimpse of blue. My fingers found the tiny insect first, tracing every detail before I stooped and pressed my lips to it. Then my mouth was on the move again, kissing and tasting until neither one of us could stand it anymore.

The rest of our clothes were shed, and I came down over her, not just connecting us physically but intimately too. Our bodies danced to the same rhythm, every movement anchoring her deeper in my heart. Every cell in my body screamed: *I need you, I love you.*

I was right there on the edge preparing to free fall into ecstasy when Kenzie grabbed my face, looked me dead in the eye and whispered, "I love you, Brett." Her breathless confession was the push I needed, and as I dived over the edge, I pulled her with me.

Catching my breath, I collapsed onto the sheets next to her and immediately gathered her in my arms. The warmth of her breaths fanned my chest.

A satisfied tiredness seeped into my bones. "I'm exhausted, but I'm afraid if I go to sleep I'll wake up and find this was all a dream," I softly admitted against her hair.

Kenzie lifted her head. The sated look on her face along with the love shining in her eyes nearly did me in. "This," she waved her finger between us. "You and me, we are the dream. *My dream.*" She wiggled until she could plant a kiss on my mouth. "Tell me you'll always be mine?"

A lump formed in my throat. Sh*e remembers*. I swallowed it down. "Forever," I vowed against her lips. "I'll love you forever, Kenzie."

The warmth of the rays filtering in through the slits in the blinds breezed over my face, my smile still firmly in place. We'd managed to sleep for all of two hours before we woke up and made love all over again. We had years of catching up to do, and I couldn't wait.

I opened my eyes and looked at Kenzie's sleeping form next to me; half tempted to slide down her body and give her a proper wake-up call. Instead, I brushed a few strands from her face and dropped a kiss to her forehead.

She stirred at the contact, her lids fluttering open revealing those beautiful eyes in which I saw my future. Her groggy, "Hi," possibly one of my favorite sounds.

"Hey, Sweetheart,"

Kenzie pushed into a seated position, hugging the sheet to her chest. Her tongue snaked over her lips, and a million wild thoughts ran through my mind, but it was the look in her eyes that made me not act on any of them.

I slipped my fingers into her hair and brushed my mouth over hers in a quick kiss. "What's going on in that head of yours?"

She snuggled into my chest and began tracing the lines of my tattoo. "I really haven't thought any further than coming here." She sneaked a peek at me and scrunched up her nose, "I'm kinda out of a job."

"You are?"

Kenzie blew out a breath. "Yeah," she pushed back into a seated position. "I confronted my parents over the letters, and things just blew up."

Panic rose in my chest, as much as I loved her, I didn't want our relationship to sever hers with her parents. "Sweetheart, if you did this so we could be together, you need to know that I will pack up and leave with you right now."

She studied me for a moment before she touched her palm to my cheek, "Always so selfless." With a shake of her head, she withdrew her hand and tucked her hair behind her ear. "I need to do this. I want to find out what I'm passionate about—" her luscious lips curled into a smile, "—besides you, of course."

The woman sitting in front of me completely stole my breath. My chest filled with pride and my heart overflowed with love, all for this incredible person that was mine.

"And," she continued. "I want to stay here in Willow Creek, make memories and hopefully, babies with you." Her eyes glistened, and I had to bite back my own emotions.

I had no words; all I could do was snag her arm and pull her to me. Pressing my mouth to hers, I kissed her as if it was our first and last kiss all rolled into one. What started out as tender quickly morphed into us hungrily eating at each other.

When I flipped her onto her back, she let out a little squeal followed by a giggle. "Again? Haven't you had enough?"

I descended on her and kissed her with more vigor and urgency. Pressing my lips to every silky inch of skin. "Sweetheart," I said between kisses. "I could never get enough of you." With my body, I made a promise to cherish and keep her safe for as long as she'd let me.

When we were both thoroughly loved up, I told Kenzie about the dog I'd picked up yesterday. Her whole face lit up, and she jumped out of bed demanding we go see how she was doing.

Driving into town with Kenzie snuggled up against me filled me with so much happiness. And to think this was merely the beginning. I pulled up at the clinic. Reaching out, I curled my fingers around her wrist to keep her from climbing out.

"Marry me?" The thought had barely formed before I was uttering the words. But it felt so right as if the past twelve years were leading up to this. Maybe I should have waited until I could've done something spectacularly romantic?

However, the smile on Kenzie's face told me a scene wasn't necessary. "It's a given," she gave me a little shrug. "Can we go see the dog now?"

I threw my head back and laughed. Man, life with this woman was going to be epic.

Epilogue

BRETT

"YOU NERVOUS?"

At Logan's question, my gaze shifted from the hall down which Kenzie had disappeared, back to him. My smile was genuine when I said, "Not even a little. Is that normal?"

My friend pulled up his shoulders, "I dunno, man. You're kinda beating me to the punch here."

"Yeah, I know," a laugh rumbled through my chest. I pulled my shoulders to my ears and held my palms up. "Sorry?" Yeah, I wasn't sorry one bit. When Kenzie agreed to be my wife a little over two weeks ago, I'd known making her Mrs. Carter would happen sooner rather than later.

Flynn sprinted through the living room with Dozer and Blue in tow. Once Kenzie had laid eyes on her at Chase's clinic, she'd agreed that the name I'd chosen was fitting. Luckily Blue didn't have any major damage to her leg, and, we were able to take her home a couple of days later.

I still had to pinch myself daily; it was hard to believe how drastically my life had changed in less than a month. But wasn't that how love worked? It knew no boundaries, had no regard for time. It just was.

Little Flynn's squeal of delight reached my ears, immediately I wondered how long it would be until Kenzie and I started expanding our family. I wanted little girls as gorgeous and feisty as their momma.

"You still with me, man?" Logan's snapping fingers broke through my thoughts. "Or are you already planning the wedding night?"

I laughed again—I'd done a lot of that lately—and waggled my brows, "Maybe."

He shook his head, but the smile on his lips told me my friend was pretty damn happy for me. "How goes the property search?"

Kenzie itched to do something work wise, and one day when Harper complained about needing to drive to another town just to look at wedding dresses, Kenzie got the idea to open up a bridal boutique in Willow Creek. My girl certainly had amazing business skills and seeing her use those skills was a massive turn-on.

"Yeah," I answered Logan's question and pulled my mind away from all the things about Kenzie that got my motor running. "She actually signed the lease last night."

My friend glanced at the hallway. "Well, hopefully, she opens her shop fast so my woman can get a damn dress."

As if she heard her name, Harper appeared along with Lizzy. Both of them looking mighty pleased with themselves. My pulse started ticking faster, "She ready?"

The women looked at each other, and their smiles just stretched wider. They moved as one, stepping in opposite directions to reveal what could only be described as an angel. My heart thumped faster and louder, and a ball of emotion lodged itself in my throat.

I raked my eyes greedily over the lacy white dress that ended just above Kenzie's knee and the brown leather boots on her feet. I swallowed hard as my gaze traveled back up and settled on her smiling face.

She slowly circled on the spot, and I caught a glint of something in her hair. Needing to be closer, I pushed off the couch and stalked over to her. Only when I was in front of my girl did I notice the tiny butterfly-shaped stones strategically placed in the curls tumbling over her shoulder.

I pressed my palm against my heart and let out a slow breath, "You look absolutely breathtaking."

Kenzie's smile widened and lit up my entire world, her eyes sparkled with pure happiness. She smoothed her palms over my white-button down. "So do you."

A big traditional wedding wasn't what either of us had wanted. Mrs. Jackson almost suffered a heart attack when I'd told her that Kenzie and I were planning on going down to the courthouse to let Judge McPherson marry us.

She'd given me the third degree for almost two hours straight while everyone else just sat back and enjoyed the show. Eventually, Kenzie had saved me by telling Mrs. Jackson we'd have the reception on the ranch and she had free rein to do what she wanted. At that suggestion, my girl had received a huge hug while I got the stink eye.

It warmed my heart when Kenzie had taken so easily to the people I considered family and vice versa.

"Right," Logan smacked his palms together. "Let's get you two married."

KENZIE

I stole a glance at the man sitting beside me; his fingers loosely curled around the steering wheel and this adorable goofy smile playing on his lips. In less than an hour, he was going to be my husband.

Husband.

I liked how that sounded. This day was going to be the best day of my life, I just knew it. My heart made a little dip, and I pushed the sadness away. I would have loved to have my parents there, for them to see how happy I was. I'd tried calling them a few times, but they never returned any of my calls.

I was hopeful that in time they would at the very least understand and respect my decision. I've only been in Willow Creek for two weeks, but already I felt like a new person. Not only did I have this wonderful future with Brett and Blue to look forward to, but I also had an exciting new business that I was building. I'd even managed to convince Brett to start a sculpture range that would be exclusive to *Forever After*.

Brett eased into a parking spot in front of the courthouse and took my hands in his, "You're sure this is fine? We could always do the whole big, fancy church thing."

I leaned forward and pressed a kiss to his cheek. "This is perfect."

He searched my face, and I saw all the love I felt for this man reflected in his eyes. "Better not keep the judge waiting, then." We climbed out of the truck; hand in hand we walked toward the people waiting for us.

The individuals Brett thought of as family were amazing people. They'd opened their hearts to me and welcomed me in without a second thought. Mrs. Jackson had a way about her that made me feel as if I'd been part of their circle for years, rather than a couple of weeks.

I frowned at Brett who seemed to be scanning the small group of people as though he was searching for someone. I tugged his hand. "Who are you looking for?" I asked when his eyes found mine.

For a second, my heart stood still as I saw sadness wash over his face. Then he smiled that smile of his that always melted all my worries away. "No one, Sweetheart."

We were met with cheers and happiness when we finally reached the steps of the courthouse. Like the mother hen she was, Mrs. Jackson ran her hands over Brett's shoulders and picked at invisible threads. She glanced at his pants and arched a brow.

"Really? You couldn't part with your jeans for one day?"

Over his shoulder, Brett winked at me. He'd known what her reaction was going to be when I'd asked him to wear his Levi's instead of dress pants. I didn't need him to change who he was though. And my man and dress pants were not friends. Plus, he looked all kinds of delicious in those hip-hugging jeans.

I scanned over the group that came together to celebrate our happiness and even though it filled me with so much joy, my heart still pinched. Knowing it had been short notice, I didn't expect Zoe to make it. Still, it would have been great to have someone there from my side.

About to mention that maybe we should go inside, I almost jumped out of my skin when someone hugged me from behind. I turned to find my best friend wearing the exact same expression as everyone else.

Feeling all kinds of emotional, I grabbed her and pulled her in for a fierce hug. "You came."

Zoe returned my embrace, "What? Did you really think I would miss my bestie's wedding?" She stood on her toes and whisper-shouted, "But if you'd told me that the men in this town were so damn fine, I'd have been here long ago."

"I've missed you." I declared on a laugh.

Appearing to be more eager than Brett or I, Mrs. Jackson started shuffling us toward the entrance.

"Kenzie."

My heart along with my feet stilled before the slamming against my ribs verged on being painful. My gaze immediately shot to Brett. He bent down and kissed me softly. "Turn around, Sweetheart."

Nerves and who knew what else held my feet hostage. Through the whooshing in my ears, I heard Brett tell everyone to go inside and that we'd join them shortly. Zoe patted my shoulder before she joined the others. I blinked, and my parents were standing in front of me.

Brett squeezed my hand, and when I looked at him, he said, "I'll be right there," he pointed toward the entrance.

I held onto his hand for dear life. "No, don't leave me."

"I'll never leave you," he whispered against my ear.

"You look beautiful." The pride in my mother's voice felt like a shock to the system. My brain was firing off a million questions though. *Why are you here? Did you know I was getting married today? If so, who told you?*

I took in the sight before me. My parents were dressed to impress. Dad decked out in an Armani suit that probably cost more than most people made in a month. Mom was wearing a sparkly dress and heels that were sure to cause blisters. But, it was the sadness in both of their eyes that hit the hardest.

In a very uncharacteristic move, my mom elbowed my dad in the ribs. He side-eyed the woman beside him, and she glared right back. My jaw almost dropped.

"I'm sorry," my father blurted out.

It might've been only two words, but they meant so much, considering it was the first time I'd ever heard them coming from the man who'd raised me.

My mom stepped forward and awkwardly reached for my free hand, once I felt the warmth of her palm against my skin, unshed tears stung my eyes. "Kenzie," she began. "We might've gone about it the wrong way, but we only ever wanted the best for you.

We never intended for you not to feel loved or for you to think your happiness wasn't important." She glanced at my dad, "Isn't that right, Walter?"

He cleared his throat and stepped forward too. "Is it too late to start making amends?"

I didn't care about make-up or looking perfect as I allowed the tears to fall freely. "It's never too late," I croaked out as I wrapped my arms around both of them.

"No tears, it's a joyous occasion," my mother sniffled as she rummaged through her purse and produced a handkerchief.

While I wiped at my tears, I caught sight of my dad holding out his hand to Brett, "Thank you for calling us—" there was a slight pause before he added, "—son." He then placed his hand on my mother's back, and to me, he said, "You *do* look beautiful." I gaped after them as they walked into the courthouse.

Brett pressed a kiss to the corner of my mouth, "You okay, Sweetheart?"

"How did you get them to talk to you let alone come down here?"

"Doesn't matter." He wrapped me up in his warm embrace. "You only need to know that there is nothing I wouldn't do for you."

I smiled into his chest. "I'm about ready for you to make an honest woman out of me."

"Then what the hell are we waiting for."